Night Songs

By Connie Sabo-Walker

Copyright ©2008 by Connie Sabo-Walker

All rights reserved. No portion of this book may be reproduced, stored in a retrieval system, or transmitted in any form or by any means –electronic, mechanical, photocopy, recording, scanning, or other –except for brief quotations in critical reviews or articles, without the prior written permission of the publisher. Efforts have been made to research this book. The validity of any information contained herein cannot be guaranteed. Any mistakes or omissions are not meant to defame or misinform.

Published in the United States by
First Stone Publishing, Inc., 8987 E. Tanque Verde #309 Box 392, Tucson, Arizona 85703 - Or visit our website: www.firststonellc.com

First Stone book titles may be purchased in bulk for education, business, fundraising, or sales promotional use. For information, please email sales@ firststonellc.org or tlc@dakotacom.net

All Scripture quotations, unless otherwise indicated, are taken from the King James Version.

Library of Congress Catalog-in-Publication Data

Walker, Connie-Sabo.
   Night Songs / Connie Sabo-Walker
   p.cm.
Includes bibliographical references.
   ISBN 13: 978-1-4276-2964-7 (pbk.)
   1.   Fiction—General. 2. Social Science—Customs & Traditions. 3. Historical—Autobiography. I. Title. II. Title: Night Songs.

Library of Congress Control Number: 2008921955

Printed in the United States of America
06 07 08 09 10 RRD 9 8 6 7 5 4 3 2

First Edition

Dedication

To my parents, sisters, and brother, who loved me and made our home happy and a safe haven growing up.

To my loving husband, Dean: a humble, gentle man. Filled and overflowing with faith. Teaching me through the years to always trust and believe the grace of God.

This is written for my children, grandchildren and great-grandchildren and loving family and friends.

And to my friend, Barbara Baer, who despite her own physical pain, edited, proof read and typed the entire first draft of this book from hand-written notes, which took the patience of the Saints to decipher!

Acknowledgments

To Sergeant First Class (Retired) Daryl Jensen – For information on Decorations of Valor during Congressional Declarations of War

To Janette Oke - An Author who is a personal inspiration to me

To Mr. Benjamin Lane – For his big heart; asking for nothing, he gave thoughtfulness, time and much needed computer skills expertise. Much gratitude.

Biblical References

John 15:13   Isaiah 11:6   Isaiah 30:29   Psalms 42:8   Proverbs 3:24

To God be all the glory,

Connie Sabo-Walker – May 2002

About the Author

Connie Sabo-Walker was born and raised in Kalamazoo, Michigan in 1941, and is the youngest of five siblings. Sabo-Walker left her beloved trees and lakes, close-knit family and the rural landscape behind to strike out on her own. Despite her innocence, and armed with nothing more than curiosity and youthful ambition, she enlisted in the Armed Services. Eventually her God-given musical ability led her into a long and diverse singing career.

Despite the demands of raising children, Sabo-Walker managed to sing in clubs, as well as in several locally produced off-Broadway musicals such as *Camelot* and *Stop the World: I want to Get Off!* For many years, her post child-rearing era singing schedule was filled with benefit concerts at convalescent homes and correctional facilities.

A singer by gift and choice, a fair painter by skill and practice – *Night Songs* is her first published work.

Today, Connie Sabo Walker lives in Tucson, Arizona, with her husband Dean, near to three of her four married children and six grandchildren. She enjoys listening to music, painting and fishing.

Much like the lead character in her book, Sabo-Walker's greatest love, is experiencing her forested environs in wintertime. To her, snow brings invigoration and exuberant joy. During snowstorms she can be found, out walking or just sitting on a snow bank for hours on end. She has even been known to make a snow angel or two!

Table of Contents

Section A - Prologue   25

Section B – Night Songs

1	Chapter One	27
2	Chapter Two	33
3	Chapter Three	37
4	Chapter Four	43
5	Chapter Five	47
6	Chapter Six	49
7	Chapter Seven	53
8	Chapter Eight	57
9	Chapter Nine	61
10	Chapter Ten	65
11	Chapter Eleven	69
12	Chapter Twelve	73
13	Chapter Thirteen	77

14	Chapter Fourteen	85
15	Chapter Fifteen	89
16	Chapter Sixteen	93
17	Chapter Seventeen	97
18	Chapter Eighteen	101
19	Chapter Nineteen	105
20	Chapter Twenty	111
21	Chapter Twenty-One	115
22	Chapter Twenty-Two	121

Section C – Conclusion

24	Chapter Twenty-Three	129

Prologue

Prologue

Mosquitoes buzz incessantly. Chiggers slip into the skin unnoticed until the itching starts. In the summer, the heat and humidity are only bearable for a short while.

The winter wetness chills the bones of the very hardy. It's an area used as a quick get-a-way for fishing or picnics. Most stay one day and leave for their homes.

Almost all are outsiders or townsfolk……..

Most……… BUT NOT ALL

Chapter One

Joe liked where he lived. He couldn't remember a time when he even thought of going anywhere else. He was a young boy when he and his Pa moved there. He also remembered that day, when Pa came and told him that his Mama couldn't hang on anymore with her sickness, and died. He didn't understand that she wasn't coming again.

They had a house in the small town about thirty miles away. He remembered the sweet smells coming from the kitchen, and her soft arms holding him. She had a way of smoothing down his hair with her hand. When he cried or needed to be comforted, he would climb up on her lap in her rocking chair. Even as he got a little bigger, she always had the time to hold him. He would bury his head in the soft sweet smelling nape of her neck and everything would be all right. How could she not be coming home again?

He also recollected their old truck loaded with most of their belongings, and driving away from there. It seemed like a long way before they stopped, rolling up to an old shack that was to become their home, the shack, and the swamp.

The air was heavy with a soft mist that even today brought him pleasure and comfort. He even talked to the place (the shack) where he now lived. He would wake up most mornings saying, "Good morning shack". He laughed aloud to think of a man with slightly Grayish hair, like himself, talking to walls and floors. What started out to be a dilapidated old "Shack," was now a pretty home, due to a lot of hard work by both of them.

Things that Joe thought was important and right, he learned from his Pa. He did go to school, his Pa wanted to make sure he could read and write and keep up with the world. Getting to school was the hard part. The truck quit running not long after they moved there, so the only way to get supplies and go to the school, was this long dugout that came with the shack. Joe couldn't wait to climb into it, hunker down, and hang on as Pa guided it through the swamp. When they first moved there, Joe had no idea that for the rest of his life, his home would be in the middle of a swamp.

Pa was a hard worker. Although he didn't work in town, word spread very quickly that he could fix and repair all most anything. On some mornings there would be work that needed fixing, neatly stacked in front of the shack. Pa would charge a fair fee for his efforts. If it couldn't be saved, there was no charge, no matter how long it took Pa to try. Spare parts were collected from here and there, and he kept those things in order, quick to find if he needed something. He was known for his honesty. His word meant trust, a rare and wonderful attribute. Pa lived his life by the Book. It was His Book, the Holy Bible. He raised Joe that way also, and the name Crocker was well known in the swamp and town.

As a small boy, Joe knew his Pa had faith. His child's mind wasn't sure what that meant, but he did know the pride he felt those few times in town. Respect was what Pa gave and

received back. Complaints were rare from Pa, as was self- pity. Any mistakes that Joe made were handled by Pa with kindness, yet firmness. Turning to the Scriptures, he would teach Joe behavior that was acceptable and honorable.

Pa was also a fine crafts man, and his Cabinet Making skills admired by many. He taught Joe, even as a small boy, how to work with his hands. Pa had no fancy tools, but he had a feel on how to mold, carve and smooth the wood.

Poling and fishing they took to with a relish. Pa made do with what tackle they had and he had a way of just knowing what to do, to catch their supper. Days and evenings were spent with the sweet smell of the swamp. Mist would rise up, and disappear into the overhead trees, giving the appearance that the branches were fading in and out.

In the evenings, there were just the two of them, sitting around the table sharing food, stories and reading the Word together. Joe was learning lessons that he didn't realize. Lessons from his Pa, the worker, teacher, counselor, friend and role model, that influenced him all of his life. Growing up to be like him was what Joe wanted the most in his life.

Lovingly Joe called his home the "swamp", which it really wasn't. It was a winding, twisting eddy, with colored water, a large river that could look black, but suddenly burst forth with Gold, Blue and Green hues, all blending into a Majestic rainbow.

Living there was a privilege. Town folks came on the weekends to fish or picnic, and they hated to leave this beautiful area, but they had no choice. There were no jobs, and no way to make a living, except fishing.

Peace and solitude were Joe's gift from God. It was not easy there. Heavy rains brought the threat of water pressing toward the shack, and having the back porch nesting on the banks, sometimes made a soggy kitchen floor. Pa would sand bag during these occasions. Both would mop up, still being happy to be there. Child hood for Joe was safe and secure with Pa. Money was scarce, but living there, and being loved, made Joe feel rich.

As time went by, Radio and Television would be all over the area, but Pa was never interested in the worldly stuff. They spent their time listening to the **night songs**, and that's what Joe liked the best. Pa was teaching him different sounds and what they meant, and those lessons kept them healthy and alive, in what could be a dangerous place to live, a place where they were the happiest.

They didn't have any neighbors. The closest people they knew were almost three miles down the bank by boat, and even longer down the dusty path some called a road. He didn't know them, and didn't think he wanted to, all he knew that it was a family with a lot of kids. He thought maybe seven or eight, but he couldn't be sure. He wouldn't have even known about anyone, except for the day he saw two small figures by the bank, as he went fishing one day.

He didn't know who was more scared as they saw each other. He jumped a little as they grabbed a rope of fish from the water, and ran like the dickens, disappearing into the heavy over grown Ferns and Bushes. Joe continued fishing that day until Sunset and headed back for the shack. He was anxious to share the news with Pa about the swamp 'creatures'.

They both had a good laugh while they cleaned and cooked the catfish he caught. Joe finished his schoolwork and put it away for the morning. He and Pa went out and sat on the back porch quietly listening to all the night songs before they went to bed. They had their Prayer time to end their day together and Joe hustled off to sleep.

It had been a while since Joe reached under his cot and took out a small Tin box that belonged to his Pa. He opened the lid, and inside the box were things that his Pa had kept. Joe called to his Pa, asking him if it was all right to see what was in the box. Pa was visibly shaken as he lifted the lid himself. Talking about the contents began a sorrowful time for both of them. The Articles of the things that were in there couldn't be explained in a short time. For about a week or more, Pa unfolded the story of a War and a life so horrible, Joe was sure his Pa had made it up.

Joe learned about War at school, but those were words in a book; now his Pa was going to tell and show him first hand. Inside the box were shinny Medals, letters, money made of coins and paper that Joe had never seen. Also in that box, were three long bullets that were bent, stained with blood, and used. Seeing those bullets connected in Joe's memory, the three big scars he had seen from time to time, on his Pa's back.

Joe discovered his Pa had another wife and daughter long before Joe and his Mama came about. They were from a Foreign Country where his Pa had served during the war. The small village where they lived was friendly to America, and his Pa met her there. They fell in love, married, and had a pretty baby girl with Black hair and deep Brown eyes. That made his story even more interesting, since Joe had Blue eyes and Copper Penny Red hair.

It was a pretty place, despite the bombing and shelling of her village. Pa and his Army buddies were stationed there, to protect the whole town as best as they could. Supplies, food and ammunition were scarce for them; but the people in this small

little place lavished all the love they had for the American soldiers.

One particularly bad day of heavy shelling, Pa's wife and baby girl were killed in the cellar they were hiding in. Joe watched his Pa cry as he told of finding them, and most of the villagers, wiped out by the bombs. Pa never took the box out again after telling Joe everything he could remember and Joe never asked him to. He watched the tears fall down his Pa's face, and held him in his arms. He had held his Pa at the cemetery, when his Mama died, and now at this time also.

Chapter Two

 Joe grew many inches the next few years, and before he knew it, he was a strapping Seventeen year old. He had been so busy during those years, he didn't think of the birthdays as they slipped by. He and Pa spent those years fishing, hunting, and growing closer together. His Pa didn't like to hunt, and his eyes showed that sadness, when he would bring home something he shot. It was necessary, once in a while, to put more food on the table, and fur for warmth during the colder times, when they couldn't get into town.

 Joe didn't like to venture into the town, even with his Pa. It was noisy and dirty, not like home. The boys that were Joe's age were mostly hooligans, looking for trouble. There wasn't much for them to do except get into fights, and Joe wanted no part of that. Not that he couldn't hold his own, he didn't like hurting anyone, and was more at peace in the shack and swamp.

 They had gone to a little church that sat on the bank of the swamp, not too far from home. It was a nice place, but they found comfort at their "own' special place of Worship, so they continued to read and study the Bible, together, at their shack. It was where they could concentrate on what was actually written and not what others thought It meant. Their solitude interrupted, sometimes by an occasional truck going down the dirt road, or a small motorboat going by, didn't change the feeling that they were in the Lord's Presence.

Pa did have a special thing he did every weekend for as long as Joe could remember. On a shelf in the kitchen, above the small sink, was where he kept his black, worn, leather Bible. His Pa would wake up, change into clean clothes, take the Bible and go off into the swamp by himself, coming home close to sundown. Nothing would interfere on that day for his Pa.

Joe once followed him to see where he went. About two miles into the meadow was a Man-Made den surrounded by bushes and ferns. It was beautiful there, and Pa would go in, sit down and just read. Joe felt ashamed of himself for following his Pa without asking, so he left quietly and never did that again. He knew that all he had to do was to ask, and Pa would have included him. He would have been disappointed that Joe was not open about what was on his heart, and had taken to deception.

Joe love the summer months. He had graduated early from High School and was looking forward to fishing and working with Pa on cabinets. He spent early mornings going along the swap bank and meadow looking for traps set by others. These weren't ones set for catching food to eat, these were traps set for pure cruelty. Traps meant to main and destroy creatures that weren't harmful to anyone. He would usually come back in time for coffee with Pa before breakfast, but knowing that he could disarm a trap, and leave it, without alerting anyone, didn't erase the ugliness of the trap itself. Pa was proud that Joe was so adept. Not even those who set the traps could tell a human hand had touched them, and this prevented angry hunters from retaliation.

One day Pa took the dugout to town for supplies. This time Joe stayed home and went fishing, because he was trying to catch a little extra fish to put on the Smoker. This would help to store up food for the cooler weather approaching. Usually Pa came home long before Sunset; but as the sky grew darker, Joe got a restless feeling. He went out on the little porch several times, looking down the swamp for the dugout to come around the bend. That night the songs of the swamp were not soothing to Joe. Fireflies, that normally caught his eye, weren't noticed. The night songs, usually bringing calmness, seemed hushed and quieter to Joe.

Finally about three hours after the sun was gone and only the stars were out, Joe heard the familiar plunk of the pole, as his Pa slowly slid up to the small dock and porch. Joe had been sitting on a stool there, waiting. He helped Pa tie up the dugout, and to Joe's surprise, had to take his hand and help him climb out. Joe took the few supplies into the shack, following Pa as close as he could. He didn't want to show any outward signs of concern. His Pa sat down in the old rocker that had been Joe's Mama's, and since became his Pa's. Joe put the supplies away, always glancing at his Pa from time to time. The silence was so loud that Joe could hear his own heart beat.

Joe knew it was not time to break that silence, no matter how much he wanted to. He put on a pot of coffee and soon the strong aroma filled the shack. Joe poured his Pa a cup, as well one for himself. Pa took the cup with a slight shake in his hand. He had almost finished drinking the whole cup, before he realized how hot it was. Joe noticed tears in his Pa's eyes, and thinking it was the heat from the coffee, let out a little chuckle.

Pa's head snapped up to look at Joe. The lungs in Joe's chest moved in and out but suddenly he could not find any air to put in them. His Pa's eyes looked so deep into his eyes, that Joe could feel the hair on the back of his neck stand up. He felt cold and hot at the same time.

The only other time Joe could remember feeling this way, was the time he was in the dug-out, and sitting next to him was a coiled up Cotton Mouth snake. He and Joe sat there, neither moving. Joe could see the skin on the snake going up and down, so he knew he was alive. Joe was sure that he, himself, never took another breath or moved, for what seemed like an eternity. As Joe sat down, it was just before noon, and it wasn't until the rays of Red and Gold filled the sky in the west that the snake decided to leave. Joe waited, not moving, while the snake crawled over his right arm and back into the water.

His Pa's eyes held Joe motionless, in the same way, as Joe held his coffee cup next to his mouth, and no further. Finally Pa spoke, "Son, the killing and bombing has begun again. War is upon the world. While you and I have been happy and safe here at the swamp, our Country has been unselfishly sending troops to a different Country, that needs our help. Almost a month now."

Pa sat back in his rocker and put his head in his hands and wept. Joe, who had been holding his back stiffly, could finally get some air and breathe again. What was his Pa telling him? It couldn't be happening. Our country was catching up on its debts, people were laughing and happy again at times. Joe realized he and his Pa had climbed into their little corner of their world and never even looked as far as their neighbors, to see if they needed help.

Pa stood up, went into his bedroom, and washed his face, then changed into clean clothes. Reaching up on the shelf in the kitchen, he took his Bible and left softly. It was only then Joe realized it wasn't the weekend. Joe did the same as Pa, and he walked into the meadow, into the small area of Prayer his Pa had made years before. Joe sat quietly a few feet away. Pa looked up and began to read aloud. That day, Joe heard his Pa speak like he had never heard his voice before. As the sun set, they both got up and walked side by side, back to the shack they called home. As they rounded the bend and caught sight of it, they both paused in unison, and then they slowly continued into the door. Each knowing nothing would ever be the same for a long time; if ever.

Chapter Three

The next morning Pa got up, and repeating the previous day, went to his place to read his Bible. Joe waited until he left, had some coffee, and began a day like no other for him. Usually if something needed fixing, Joe would get to it sooner or later, but not this day. Joe worked on anything and everything that he could see, or remember, needed to be taken care of. Sweat poured from every inch of his skin. He stopped only long enough to quench his thirst. Food never entered his mind, and if it did, a wave of nausea accompanied it. He was so intent and busy that it was only when he felt his Pa's hand on his shoulder, did he stop. By now he had been working by moonlight. He never heard the night songs that had been reaching out to him.

Joe skipped eating but did have a cup of coffee with Pa. Then he stumbled into his bed, bone weary. He thought he would sleep, but it wouldn't come. He tossed and turned so much that by morning he was even sorer than when he threw himself down on his mattress. He heard Pa in the kitchen and soon could smell the coffee, even bacon and eggs cooking.

Joe, like when he was a small child, opened his window and slid out quietly; down to the cool water of the swamp. He scrubbed his skin until it started to tingle, and red blotches appeared. Joe got out, toweled off, put on his fresh clothes and went in the porch door. His eyes met with Pa's. and without a word, they both hugged and sat down together. Joe couldn't think of a time when breakfast or any other meal tasted so good.

Joe finished and stood up, hugged his Pa again, and went out the door. Slowly and carefully he got into the dugout. He stood tall and lifted the pole. Turning his head, he saw his Pa. He was sitting on the same stool that Joe had sat on awhile back. Joe pushed off and headed for town. They both knew what he was going to do without so much as a word passing between them. Joe banked the dugout as close to town as he could, and walked the three miles more. The town and the people acted different. So did Joe.

It didn't take long to reach the Army recruiting office. It took even less time to enlist, get his orders and head back home to pack. Two days later his Pa was hugging him so hard, he thought his ribs would break. He knew his heart had.

The first year of the War, for Joe, was like his Pa had told him. The memory of opening the mysterious box under his bed many years ago now haunted him. What he thought would be a treasure, was opening a box of horror and doom. Joe also went back in his mind, how he had doubted the recollection of his Pa. "Nothing could be that terrible" is what his tender heart had said, and now Joe was there, in that box, along with his Pa.

Joe's outfit was big and mostly impersonal. He would find a friend one day, and the next day, sadly, that new friend would die in his arms. This was incomprehensible and unbearable to even think about, but forgetting and putting it out of his mind was impossible.

Joe did like the men on his squad. They were tight knit and worked well together. He was amazed to find out that his Sergeant, was one of the older brothers, of the two young kids he saw fishing that day at the swamp. They were both from "home". They spent what free time they had, sharing and swapping stories of their hometown. Joe would laugh to himself, as the Sergeant would talk of "His swamp" this and that. After all, the swamp, shack and night songs were Joe's, and not anyone else's.

The first year of the War now stretched to three. Joe and the Sergeant shared each and every letter from home. Joe's Pa wrote at least three times per week, but the Sergeant, with so many at his home, out did everyone. What with the troops moving constantly, sometimes the mail didn't catch up with the men for weeks. You always knew mail call in Joe's squad, by the shouts and laughter. The Sgt's mail filled two to three bags alone, and he got used to the men taking hands full first to read, then giving the mail back to him.

Many long and lonely nights, the men would share and read some of those letters out loud. It wasn't very often they were secure enough to speak out loud in the evenings, but when it was, they would all the would huddle around the fire, taking turns, picking out the Sgt's moving, and often funny, stories of back home and the swamp.

Joe was beginning to start to write to the Sgt's sister, whose name was Sara. Joe was struck by her writing. She seemed to capture the same feelings of living at the swamp that Joe had. He found himself talking to the Sergeant about her. He was cautious, because, he didn't want it to appear that he had more than a casual interest in her. Joe was too busy staying alive, helping to keep the men of the squad from death's door.

Thinking of home and Sara was sometimes more than he wanted in times like this.

The Sergeant and Joe were especially effective during the night watch. They had a system of sounds, known only by the two of them. To communicate and forward important information to the Higher Ranks, much faster than the usual Walkie-Talkies that were handed out. More than a dozen times they picked up hidden ambushes and traps, sending the info on ahead; saving the men of their squad from sure death. When asked what the sounds meant and how to teach others, they could not. It wasn't that they didn't try. How can you teach others, what you knew from childhood about all of those wondrous night songs of home, the shack, and the swamp?

A few months later the camp was filled with news of a "Secret" Weapon soon to arrive. Their squad was singled out to receive this weapon because of their successes, always being one step ahead of the enemy. This Weapon had been used before in previous Wars, but not in this one, that is not until now. The men had no idea of what was in store for them, how this "secret" would affect them all. Not only for now, but long after this war ended, if it ever would.

As usual with the Military, time dragged on and it was day by day, keeping alive, moving and more moving. Letters did manage to find them and thankfully, kept the men connected to home. "Home" – was the word that brought comfort to the men.

By now as the years went by, each man in the squad received a Bible. Some from the Army but most came from home, from family. Joe had gotten his from Pa about six months after leaving. He remembered the day it arrived. He opened the box, thinking it was a little heavy for cookies, and so happy to receive it. Wrapped securely in his Pa's favorite flannel shirt, was the same Bible Joe remembered his Pa taking down from the shelf over the kitchen sink. Joe found a distant, private place, put the Bible in his arms, and with tears in his eyes he couldn't control, rocked back and forth clutching it to his heart.

Joe had read and reread the Bible many times in his short life. Some of which he understood and some he didn't. All he knew for sure was during the unbearable, heart stopping moments, of this time and place, he would find himself searching in his memory, for the Words that kept him going, wanting to stay alive, and wracked with guilt watching those who weren't.

He found that writing to Sara also helped. She and Joe would discuss many things, and he would sometimes ask her about what he had read, for the meanings. She would explain as best as she could. Having her express her Beliefs and thoughts was bringing them closer together, although Joe didn't realize it as much as Sara did.

What a day!!! The men couldn't believe their ears. They were told that they had possibly two weeks of rest coming to them. You could hear the hoots and hollering resound around the camp. They had just arrived there the day before, and were totally worn out, afraid that this was just a stop over to the next Battle line. Instead of enjoying a good night sleep, warm and dry; one or more would be up, scouting the perimeter, hunkered down next to a tree or up in it, peering down on the sleeping camp. Always on watch, forgetting that this time they could rest, and so they appeared more haggard than the night before.

With the men moving around so much, taking as little as possible could mean the difference between life and death. The Bible was never left behind. There were times, when the squad had no warning notice of Enemy fire, that escaping barely happened. As time went on, more and more of those times enveloped them.

Now finally a rest, getting a chance to recuperate, replaced by a fresher, just "off the boat" troop. A welcomed report for all involved. As they marched back to where headquarters were, they passed the ones to take over. Joe couldn't get over how young and "baby-faced" this group was. His heart hurt for them; knowing the next time he saw them, they would never be the same again. Growing up would be as instantly violent for them as all who marched and fought for their country before. It wouldn't take too long, not here, not now.

After a few days the men got "new" mail. It was great to take time and have the peace to read and reread each one. Joe got his usual one from Pa. He sounded like he was doing all right, but Joe got a lump in his throat when he read that his Pa had taken a fall. He said it was nothing to worry over, that he hadn't broken any bones, and was just sore for a few days. Joe suddenly had this ache in his heart for him and home. He wanted to go home right then and there. To get in the dugout, hang his arms over the side and watch his Pa move slowly and quietly through the swamp. Their swamp; No matter how the Sergeant would say it was "his", Joe took claim on it that day after the letter from Pa.

He quickly sat down and wrote Sara. He had never asked her to go over and checkup on him before. His Pa didn't take kindly to strangers coming over. Not that he was unfriendly or menacing, it was just that Pa seemed to like the idea, that any visiting would be in town, when he went for supplies, and so only his closest friends came to their home at the swamp.

Joe suddenly couldn't bare it. He needed his shack and mostly the night songs.. Just like the time Pa told him of the war and he felt helpless and scared. This time it seemed worse. Joe was younger then, he could manage to recoup after a few days of hard work or excitement, this time he couldn't.

4
Chapter Four

Chapter Four

What about Pa? Who was there for him now? What if he went down and no one found him? Joe couldn't wait for a letter to reach him. He wanted to know now, but they had no phone. Joe had wanted put one in, but when the Telephone Company went out there, Pa gently told them "no thanks" and sent them away. Joe even laughed when he received his money back. The check was still in his wallet, but now it wasn't funny. Nothing was funny.

Joe wasn't sure what to do. He looked around for the Sergeant, maybe he would know. He found him behind the mess tent, reading his mountain of mail. Joe stood there for a while, he didn't want to intrude on the smiles the Sergeant had on his face. Finally the Sergeant looked up to see Joe standing there. He knew by the look on Joe's face it was pretty important and he motioned for Joe to have a seat.

Joe explained the letter and his fear for his Pa. He asked the Sergeant if he knew what to do and how to do it. After what seemed like an eternity for Joe, the Sergeant got up and told Joe what he had in mind. As they headed for the Chaplain's tent, Joe wasn't sure what he could do either, but he trusted the Sergeant, even though they weren't but a few years apart in age.

They were invited in right away. Joe explained the situation and the Chaplain asked them to give him a little time and he would get back with them. Meanwhile mail call came, and Joe gave his letters to the mail clerk, two for Pa and the "special" one for Sara. The Sergeant knew the fear in Joe's eyes. He had had the same look many times back home.

His own life was hard at home, being the third of twelve children. His oldest brother had already given his life for his Country. His heart held many scars from the past, and now here, in this strange, distant Country, new scars had formed. He sure hoped there was some way to help Joe. God knew he tried his best back home and now here.

His mind wandered back to when his pretty sister Emily had gotten the measles, and how he helped his own Father lay her in the grave, not too far from their home in the swamp. And pretty Sara, lying in bed with Polio, and not expected to live, but never without her unfailing Faith and devotion to God. The Sergeant couldn't remember a time when she didn't have a smile on her face, a helping hand for others. Her struggle to learn how to walk again, weighed down with heavy cumbersome braces.

His heart swelled with pride remembering her determination and will, to conquer the pain of lifting and using the withered thin legs. Not only did Sara conquer that illness, she was always running and skipping with those "things" on her legs, and that was a sight to behold.

The Sergeant did notice that she and Joe had spent a lot of time writing to each other. He never asked to read those letters. He also noticed Joe inching his way up to the front of the mail call line, fidgeting around until his name was called. His eager hand held out, not only for his Pa's letter, but held up high in case there was a letter from Sara, which there always was. Later that day, during evening "Mess" call, the Chaplain found the Sergeant and Joe, and sat down to talk to them. He had been a busy man and after rechecking Joe's letter from home, he got both their files to study them. He thought he had found a solution and was anxious to tell them.

Joe and the Sergeant gave their full attention to his every word. When the Chaplain finished, there were a few moments of silence he wasn't prepared for. Finally they both stood up, grabbing the Chaplains arms and did a dance all around the table where they had been sitting. They all made quite a scene for about five minutes or longer, much to the surprise and shock of the other soldiers.

It had been a long time to see happiness of any kind and it was welcomed. Before anyone could stop them, the whole mess tent erupted in hooting, hollering and dancing. It didn't matter much that the men didn't know why they were caught up in a moment of glee and it wasn't long for reality to catch up to them. One by one they sat down, a little red in the face, but still smiling.

The Chaplain, Joe and the Sergeant headed for the communications bunker. As the Chaplain had told them earlier, after checking, he found out the Sergeant was the only one who had a phone. After explaining to his Major, what he thought was a possible serious home matter for one of the two men, he was given permission for a call to be placed at the Sgt's home. He had assumed, they being neighbors, they would have information about Joe's Pa.

According to the Major, the word "neighbor" meant living in row houses in the city, and neither Joe, or the Sergeant, dreamed of saying anything to the contrary. It didn't matter to them that in actuality they lived miles apart in a swamp, their families barely knowing about each other.

The phone call had to be made within the hour, due to the time difference and security reasons. The "go ahead" was given to the Clerk, from the Chaplain, and He got busy on the square canvas box. It had a turn crank, and he began a series of turns and twists. Next came an unseen person on the other end for a list of connecting stations. All this was taking a long time and Joe found himself pacing back and forth but the Sergeant stood mesmerized by all the action.

It had been over a year since he had heard a family members voice. The last time was when his brother had lost his life, and the grief on both ends of the line still left a lump in his throat. He prayed that whoever answered the phone wouldn't think it was more terrible news, especially his parents. He didn't know if they could take the call thinking he was wounded or worse.

    At last they heard the clerk exclaim, "Please hold on for a phone call from Sergeant Garrity". With a shaky hand, the Sergeant took the receiver and said "hello", it's me and I'm alright". He was glad when he heard the sweet voice of his sister Sara calling his name. They laughed and talked for about five minutes when the clerk held up his hand with four fingers sticking out. The Sergeant got right to business, listening with a surprised look on his face. From what Joe could put together, she not only knew, but was also going over to Joe's Pa house, twice a week, to check up on him and visit with him.

    She had never mentioned this to Joe or the Sergeant in any of the letters. Joe heard the Sergeant say "good-by", and then, the phone was in his hand. Suddenly Joe caught on, and with a croaky, high-pitched voice, spoke to Sara for the first time. Her voice matched the vision Joe had in his mind. It was soft but strong, younger than he imagined, but none the less very beautiful.

Chapter Five

    They barely said a few sentences before the clerk held up one finger. No, no, not yet, he thought. By the time Joe told Sara they only had one minute more, she was gone. Sara's voice was gone. Joe held on to the receiver even though the clerk was pulling on it. Joe's attention was back to reality now and slowly he handed the phone back to him. Try as he might, his feet wouldn't move. All of a sudden he felt like a thirteen year old hick who had just said "hello" to a girl for the first time.

    Sheepishly, Joe followed the Sergeant outside. He knew there was a smirk on the clerk's face. His mind was on all the things the Sergeant and Sara talked to each other about, especially Pa. Once back in the fresh air, Joe felt better; walking with the same confidence he had before the phone call. At least he wasn't acting like a yokel, with his toe kicking the dirt, mumbling, "oh shucks".

    The Sergeant pretended not to notice Joe's embarrassment and they went back to the mess tent. He wanted to fill Joe in on all he and Sara had talked about. On the walk back, they were both pretty quiet. Each caught up in the past few minutes, and the thought of home. The Sergeant reached into his top shirt pocket, opened a brown worn wallet. He handed Joe a picture. It was of Sara.

Joe and the Sergeant had plenty of time to talk and get to know each other over the past year or so. They talked mostly of home, the swamp and the night songs. They both agreed it was so much more than that. There was a beauty there that was hard to describe. Water at times was so clean and clear, you could see all the way to the bottom. Fish, crawdads and wavy grass that looked like it was dancing. Also in that water, besides being clear in spots, was muddy, Brown, murky areas, holding scary mysteries.

Hidden dangers, like the many types of snakes living there. They were soft, shinny, friendly snakes, which would curl around your hand, with their tongues darting in and out. Then there were the ones that would try to get into the dugout, striking with fangs dripping with poison. They both had "near miss" stories and admitted at times they scrambled and ran faster than they thought they could.

Chapter Six

There was a question on the Sgt's mind about Sara. He wondered if she ever told Joe about her Polio and her legs. If she did, Joe never mentioned it to him, and if she didn't tell Joe, he was wondering why she kept that part of her life hidden. Sara was the most truthful, honest person he knew, but those were the type of questions he would not pursue. Privacy was important to her, and only she and Joe had those answers. He would respect that.

Before the war, Joe had dated a few times, no one special though. He loved fishing and being in his special world of the swamp. After all, who needed more than that? There had been a girl he saw six or seven times. She appeared nice, was well educated, and came from a nice home. She seemed to really want to continue seeing Joe. He on the other hand, felt he had to be and act like someone he wasn't. He always saw a disinterested look on her face when he would start talking about where and how he lived. She thought it was "cute" when he would call his Father "Pa". Joe lost all feeling he might of had for her , when she said she could never live near a swamp. That it would be creepy and too far from civilization, culture and the fine arts, she was use to being around and couldn't live without.

Joe now found himself thinking only of Sara; when he wasn't moving around and trying to stay alive. He would take her picture, the one the Sergeant had given him, and look at it a lot. It was just a snapshot off her from the shoulders up. It was in Black and White, so at first Joe didn't know what color her hair or eyes were.

Joe did manage, without seeming too interested, to find out from the Sergeant, more about her. She had Honey Brown hair, eyes that were Hazel with Golden flecks in them. She was five feet, two inches tall, and couldn't weigh more than an arm full. According to the Sergeant, her soft laughter, which she shared with all who knew her, filled the hearts with warmth, that couldn't be copied or described.

Joe just thought the Sergeant was partial until the day Joe actually heard her voice on the phone; such a short, almost non-existent conversation. It brought about feelings for Sara, Joe didn't know he had, not until this very moment. Here in this far away, harsh, Day after Day, trying to stay alive, Country. He was far away from the shack, the swamp, Pa and now, Sara.

Sara, who was from the same Home Town, loved it there, never even mentioning any other place she wanted to go to be. Most of all, Sara, who like Pa, wanted Joe to come back to a shiny fixed up place. She was comfortable in the dugout, fishing, laughing, and hearing the night songs. His, Pa's, and now hers: night songs of home.

Joe wasn't sure if he was feeling happy or annoyed that he spent so much time thinking of Sara. After all, he was pretty sure he knew exactly what he wanted when he left there. He didn't want change. He had had enough hectic, fast moving, uncertain times in his life these past few years. All he wanted to do were the "familiar" things, with only Safety, Peace and Quiet, for himself and his Pa, picking up just where they had left off.

Sure, he had changed, matured, maybe grew up a little, but he didn't want to grow up so much and so fast, that he couldn't go back and settle in where he was, before this blasted War. The time came for Joe's squad to get some rest and relaxation (R&R). The war was heating up more and more and the dying and the wounded were being sent to where Joe's men were. There were at least three mash units always ready, and the sound of Helicopters buzzing constantly, were like the insects of the swamp.

The Sergeant, Joe and the men were anxious to get back into it, and help out their comrades as best as they knew how. To sit around and watch, and do nothing, was too much for them. They spent time getting their gear in order, checking and re-checking to make sure all their equipment was in tip-top shape to go at a moment's notice.

The mail caught up with them much faster being they were in one place for a while. Joe heard from both Pa and Sara. He read his Pa's letters first because he was anxious to read and get a "feel" for his Pa's words of home, and his health. Joe was relieved that from what he could tell, his Pa was up and around and back to his old self.

He laughed how Pa had written in the letter about the biggest catfish he had ever caught. Pa told him how it took almost two hours to bring the fish in, and that his arms hurt from just holding on to the fishing pole. Also how he almost lost it at the edge of the dugout, when it slipped off the hook, hit the pole, bounced off his knee, and finally slipped to the bottom by his feet, where he promptly sat on it.

That night, he savored the best dinner he had in a long time. Pa told Joe in his letter, that Sara had been along that day fishing with him. They had a regular day of the week, just the two of them. She would come in her dugout, and pick him up before dawn. He would "pole out" and off and they would go. He also said that Sara was the one who was teaching him how to fry catfish, so tender and sweet, that it almost melted in his mouth.

The rest of Pa's letter was all about Sara. It seems that since his fall, they both became best swamp buddies. It was Sara who would point out things that needed fixing, and Pa would get busy. Sara told Pa, "Joe will be coming home one day soon, and things should look real nice for that day." The next page of Pa's letter had Joe scratching his head. Pa was now going over every Tuesday to Sara's home.

He and her Pa had a lot in common and that particular day was checker day. He was the leader by six games, and Daniel, her Pa, met him every Tuesday morning saying "You might as well give up, today is the day when you get the worst whipping of your life". "Yes sir" said Pa, "the only thing that would make life better, was having Joe and Sara's brother home for good."

It was amazing to Joe that in all the letters he received from Sara, she never mentioned the time spent with Pa. It wasn't that Joe minded their getting close to each other, he was happy for them both. It was that he didn't have a clue, being they both were so closed mouth about it. Not that was strange, after all, back home was private and so were all the folks that lived there. That's why it was so special to have a fine place to live.

Chapter Seven

It was late and Joe was tired. It was almost lights out and the scuttlebutt had been going around: the "Secret Weapon" would be there at first light and it was about time. So many theories and guesses of just what it would be. From double the "elite troops" to bullet-proof uniforms; finally tomorrow would put an end to speculations. He prayed that night, for an end to this war, which he had done many times before. This Weapon might do it, but at what expense? What kind of suffering lay in store for them?

This far away Country's War was different than a lot of other Wars. It was this difference that made Joe remember his own beloved country. Once, It was torn in half also, brother against brother, Country-men against Country-men. There were entire families, torn apart, logistically, physically and mentally.

Joe lay down in his bunk, unable to turn off the sights and sounds he had seen, and been a part of. The war did seem to be less intense and all that talking was fine, but what about the people doing the actual fighting? The villagers were haggard, sick and starving. The faces of those along the roads haunted him. Hands were held out for any food or medicine that they could beg for. The little children and babies, their vacant eyes and bloated stomachs from starvation and pain, Joe couldn't turn it off this night. He tossed and turned for hours.

Joe's mind took him back home to his Pa. There was many a night he would lift up his head from his bed and peer down the hallway leading to Pa's room. He could still see the silhouette of him, on his knees, in Prayer. There were times, when Joe was younger, that he would pounce happily into bed, thinking of fishing, school, tomorrows' and the night songs. Then he would lift his head a certain way up from the pillow and see Pa. He would dutifully climb out of his warm, comfortable bed, and go to his knees in Prayer.

Most of the time it was from guilt that he had forgotten to Pray. He admired Pa and tried to follow his example. Joe's Prayers were the simple ones of a young growing boy. Now that he thought of it, purely selfish of the "give me this and that". Often he would grow sleepy and tired trying to stay on his knees as long as Pa did. Sheepishly he would climb back between the covers and fall asleep. Now he knew, what made Pa sometimes groan as he Prayed.

This war did seem to have reached a turning point, and talks of peace were on going, and now this "Secret Weapon." Would it be so horrendous, that the suffering and Death could never be measured, forgotten, or forgiven? Joe shivered and trembled, and his knees were numb from the weight of his body in Prayer. He slid beneath the blankets and felt his body relax a little. Perhaps sleep would come, finally.

His head kept saying to wake up, but Joe's body wouldn't respond. He could see his breath and was shivering. At first it was funny, when the time came to get winter supplies, and with the Army, requisitions were not what you expected. This time, along with six thousand toilet seats, there were just enough boots for one pair each. Not that they ever fit anyone the right way.

Joe was not too unhappy though. His boots were two sizes too big, but each man had received a dozen pairs of socks, and he could wear three pair at once, put on the boots, and his feet kept nice and warm, for now. Winter was here and although snow had been sparse, it was dipping into the teens. Joe heard that the months ahead were going to be brutal, with snow high enough to bog the men down. They would be able to get an easy fix on the enemy, but now would be prime targets themselves.

Joe shook off the sleepiness, swung his feet out and got up. He smiled to himself. He was fully dressed, boots and all. Not only saved time dressing, but could save his life when seconds counted.

His stomach rumbled, and he was hungry. Ah yes, good old Military chow: Powdered eggs, dry toast, Spam, and hot coffee. Actually he liked Spam, anyway that it was fixed. The eggs, sometimes, were cold, and usually runny, but he could make a sandwich of them and was grateful to have any food at all. Even K-rations weren't that awful considering the starving people they would encounter along some of the roads they had to foray.

Coffee! How do you explain one of the most anticipated things in the Military? Cold days or hot days made no difference. One could lose all cravings for food, but not for coffee. You never knew as it went down the throat, just exactly what it was. There was talk that it was joined, somehow, to the Oil pans kept under the jeeps. They were kept there to prevent leaving Black traces the enemy could follow. He knew the coffee rations were sparse, so mixing the two, Oil with Grinds, (in Joe's mind) seemed the logical thing for them to do. Hot it always was, but the Oil taste never left his throat.

He pretended it was just made on his stove, in his kitchen. He thanked God for all he received every day. The thought of total starvation made Joe hurry to the chow line. He picked up a tray and again, was Thankful. There was enough for two Spam sandwiches, a rare treat. He saw part of the squad and sat down with them. After a few sleepy nods of recognition, he began to eat.

Just as he started to eat his second sandwich, he felt a jab at his ankle, causing Joe to freeze. There were poisonous snakes here, but it was the wrong time of the year. A second jab hit Joe. Very slowly he lowered his eyes, without moving any part of his body, and down by his leg was a pair of Brown eyes looking up at him.

Joe let out the air he had been holding. Reaching down he patted the head of what belonged to the Brown eyes. It was a dog, but it wasn't like any of the dogs he had seen around the camp before. Most of them were scrawny, half-starved, and would run away if you tried to touch or feed them. Joe had attempted touching and petting some before, without any success, so he ended up leaving a few scrap for them before moving on.

This was a beauty of a dog. A massive head attached to a well fed muscular body. Brown with a black saddle on its back, and just a hint of blonde hairs scattered around. Joe began to stroke and pet the dog looking at him.

The tail started swinging so hard and fast it was slapping the guy next to him. Quicker than a blink, he had a lap full of dog. A big male German Shepherd, with maybe a husky blend. Even back home, with all the "left on his door-step dogs", he had never seen such a perfect animal. Big but young, and Joe could tell that by his playfulness and trust. His eyes didn't look at the food, only at Joe.

Chapter Eight

He seemed quite content in Joe's lap. The guys were calling and encouraging the dog to come to them. There were scraps of food sailing everywhere; some of it pelting Joe on his head and back. One chunk of meat slammed into Joe's ear, drawing a speck of blood. Suddenly the dog was down, across the mess hall, and on to the arm of the man that threw it. His massive jaw chomped down on it, pulling him face first, right out of the chair he was sitting in.

Then the dog sat on his haunches, his face about one inch from the scared soldier's face. The quiet in the mess hall was deafening. The poor soldier's eyes were looking for help, from all of the other eyes that were staring back at him. They seemed to be pleading for help of some kind, any kind. Then there came the sound of a cocked rifle.

Joe quietly stood up. Moving across the room, he stopped about four feet away from the two. Joe could see the big face of the dog, with his Canine teeth barred into this grotesque twisted half smile. The dog's eyes were locked unto the downed man's entire head, which despite the chilly air, was covered in sweat. Joe made a soft sound. A sound you make when you want complete silence. Just a "Shushing" sound that most of the men didn't even hear at all.

The massive head lifted up, away from the downed man, and locked eyes with Joe. Never moving his body, Joe lifted his own chin a little and the dog softly came and stood by Joe's side, still keeping an eye on the still downed, scared, sweaty soldier. Joe reached down, touched the dog's head with the palm of his hand. The dog looked up at Joe expectantly.

Without saying another word, Joe turned, dog at his side, and went back and sat down. He began to eat his now, ice-cold sandwich. Satisfied that Joe was all right, the dog sighed softly and lay down on the floor by Joe's side, still facing most of the men. The downed soldier gently eased his shaking body back into his own chair without making any sudden moves. The murmur of the men's voices began again, but instead of chatter laced with expletives, their talk now, was mostly low key talking, about what had just happened.

Joe himself had silent thoughts mulling in his own head about this wondrous creature lying by his feet. He couldn't remember a time having that happen to him or seeing it happen. He even thought it was a fluke. A one-time event that no one would believe, not even him. He knew he was chewing his food, drinking his cold, oily, coffee, but there was no noticeable taste. Joe felt his jaw moving up and down, still lost in the amazement of the last few moments.

Joe had almost finished, and out of boyhood instinct, took a small piece of the food left, and reached down to share with the new friend at his feet. Even the smell of more to eat could make the dog take his eyes from the men in the room. Joe knew then that this was not the time to distract him with anything. He was on guard, in a protection mode, that to the dog was more important than food, or anything else that would interfere with protecting Joe. For some unknown reason, tears filled the corners of Joe's eyes. He blinked them away, hoping no one would notice. He took the paper napkin by his plate, filled it with scraps, tucking it in his shirt pocket for later. A "later" he hoped would come his way. He forced himself to think, that as suddenly as the dog was in his lap, he could be gone, forever.

Joe's thoughts were interrupted by the sound of the Sgt's voice. He was walking across the room with his tray, fast approaching the both of them. The Sergeant let out an appreciative whistle to see the beautiful animal lying by Joe. The dog quickly sat up on his two front feet. He turned his head to Joe as if waiting for a "sign." And the hair on the nape of his neck began to stand up. The sound of the Sgt's voice increased the urgency in his eyes for a command from Joe. Joe again made the soft "shush" sound, only this time it had a different connotation to it. The dog's neck hairs went down and a slow wag of his tail began. The "Young" in the pup was beginning to show again. For the moment his big tongue rolled out dripping gooey drool all over the floor.

 The Sergeant sat right next to Joe, reached down and gave the dog several pats on his head. Most of the men were watching, waiting for barred teeth and another man to hit the floor. To their surprise, nothing happened. Not a growl or a snarl, just a tail wag.

 Joe had to admit it to himself, what happened before with the dog, was just what it was, a one-time strange event. He wasn't anything special to this stray. Joe's heart, felt heavy inside. He knew it was out of pure conceit and selfishness to think that he could "communicate" to this animal.

 He wanted this occurrence to be a "Miracle". A gift, a sign, something wondrous he could hold on to, in all the carnage around him. He Prayed quickly, and silently, for forgiveness in his presumption of thinking, that he was special and deserving of a "Miracle." He and the Sergeant sat and talked. Mostly about what had happened to the poor soldier, who by now had made his way out of the side door, barraged by laughter from the other men.

 Joe made no mention of what had made the dog stop attacking the guy or anything else. He just stroked the dog on the head from time to time. Finally picking his tray up to leave, he felt the need to be by himself. For a few wonderful moments the war seemed far away. Sure, there was violence right there in the mess hall, but it was the kind you would see just about anywhere in the world. A faithful pet protecting his master. The biggest and saddest difference to Joe, was, they didn't belong to one another at all.

Joe dropped his tray off and started outside, he wrapped his coat tightly around him to keep out the wind and the snow, shivering just thinking about another day of war. His hand was on the door when he felt the now familiar, jab, jab, jab, poking him on the side of his ankle. He looked down to those beautiful brown eyes, looking up at him. He was poised and waiting for Joe to direct him. A lump formed in Joe's throat. Joe knew that God had sent a miracle to him, right now, here in this place. Peace had come into his heart and soul. Touching the dog's head with the palm of his hand, he bent his own head slightly downward, and said a silent Prayer of Thanksgiving.

Chapter Nine

Joe turned his head at the Sgt's voice calling him, "Hey guys, wait for me" and the three of them walked out into the cold snowy day together. Going down the man- made road to their tent, they made quite a sight. It was hard to tell who was younger, the two men or the pup jumping and hopping along with them. Their walk turned into "tag--you're it" or "go fetch".

The Sergeant and Joe were laughing so hard and were so breathless, they fell over some Scrub Bushes. It was too much for the young dog to resist. He nosed dived the both of them, his big head nuzzling Joe's face, whacking the Sergeant on the side of the head with his wagging tail, and sending his helmet down the path like a lop-sided bowling ball.

Just then the squeak squawk of the loud speaker broke their reverie, and it was back to where they were, not where they wanted to be; reality. The un-seen voice from the speaker barked out the order for all soldiers to report to the mess hall, and there were no exceptions unless on Guard Duty.

With all the men packed into the mess hall, the wet wool over coats, mixed with evolving perspiration, started to mingle with the aroma of noon mess cooking. Some of the men started to turn a shade of color that was un-mistakable. A Greenish Hue of impending nausea. Different levels of grumbling began as time started to drag on. The doors were flung open and in came a parade of officers. Most of them were men they knew, except three High Ranking Captains and one Major.

The men came to an immediate "Attention" stance before the order was given.

The Major blew a whistle and to Joe's disappointment, the dog went quickly over to him. Turning his massive head back toward the Sergeant and Joe, he seemed to act as though time with them was gone. The spring and bounce visibly less, or so Joe thought.

The Major cleared his throat and began to speak. "Men, you all have heard the scuttle-butt of a "Secret Weapon" that was due here today. It is indeed here and whether it stays depend on the men of this camp. This is the third unit that we have been to, and frankly, the results of success so far, have been dismal.

This is an excellent search, seize and destroy Weapon. Six months of trials have proven it. My officers and I accompanied it to other units, however, in our opinions, until today, we had dismissed the viability of such a Weapon in this particular conflict". The major continued, "Every soldier so far, wants this Weapon for himself to operate and use. However, no one has been able to handle it to its full potential. That is until now". With that, the Major gave the order to dismiss and resume full muster outside for a demonstration of the "Weapon" to begin in ten minutes.

The men again went back to Full Attention Stance and watched as the officers left the mess hall, the Major, followed by the three Captains. The only difference was the dog held his stance, his gaze on Joe and the Sergeant. Upon seeing this, the Captain who held the whistle, gave a short sharp blast with it, and the dog reluctantly followed.

Most of the men grabbed a cup of coffee and went outside, except Joe and the Sergeant. They hung back without saying a word. Joe didn't know for sure what the Sergeant had on his mind but he was thinking of the dog. Sure the "secret weapon" had piqued his interest, and that was undeniable. Strangely though, his mind turned to the swamp, shack and beloved night songs. Only now, this time, it was with the dog sitting on his back porch.

Out in the fresh air once again, the two blinked their eyes and took deep breaths, almost in unison. They cleared the past minutes of stale sour air from their lungs. Walking along, neither of them said anything for a while, until the Sergeant quietly remarked, "I didn't like what I saw". Glancing at Joe, he continued. "No one treats or trains a dog like that, blowing that shrill noise hurt my ears, can you imagine what it did to the dogs?" Joe, with his jaw clinched tight, said, "you and I agree as usual". A little love goes along way".

Stopping for a minute, the Sergeant asked Joe if he wanted to call him by his first name, "Mark," when they were by themselves. Joe was grateful not only to have such a friend, but one from home. Joe recollected in his thoughts, about three men that he could say were his friends. One, a guy he met during basic training, was quite a bit older than he was. They always seemed to end up in the same camp, and it was a relief to see his face during the first roll call. They worked well together and always watched each other's backs. His death, during a night maneuver, about a year ago, always brought a pain in Joe's heart. He felt blessed to have known him. His other friend was still back home; he didn't come from the swamp, but from town. They grew up together and in school or fishing, he was a great guy to chum around with. He didn't make it to this War. He had come down with Polio. He lived his life in an "iron lung" and his battle was never going to be over. An individual war where there would be no victory except the invisible one that of his personal faith, which he shares with Joe, in a wondrous never-ending joy.

Joe was very happy and honored that the Sergeant wanted him to call his by his first name. With all the things they shared, he really felt that they were more like brothers, than just two men thrown together by circumstances. Grinning like a Cheshire cat, Joe punched him in the arm. The Sergeant punched him right back, only harder. Speaking from his heart, Joe told him, that if it would be all right with him, he would hold off from calling him Mark for now. He, out of respect, would call him "Sarge" and when they got home instead of Cpl. Crocker and Sergeant Garrity, they would be Joe and Mark.

Up ahead they saw the men stretched all around the field that was outside the camp. Joe and Sarge mingled in, starting to catch the curiosity and excitement in the air.

The area was almost as big as a football field. Besides the few trees and natural mounds of grassy dirt, Joe noticed that other things had been added. Several earthen huts, rolls of brambles, two jeeps, a truck and huddled in a small circle, a group of actual villagers cooking and talking in their native tongue. It was almost eerie, because it was a carbon copy of the jungle, mixed with occasional bareness they faced here every day.

Reality hit Joe hard. Soon, very soon excitement would be replaced with fear: curiosity with suspicion, extending a friendly hand with a pointed rifle, buddies becoming buddies. Joe's mind screamed, "stop enough". Shivering and shaking, Joe forcefully took his mind home, to the swamp, the shack, the dog, and Pa. Joe lowered his head in silent prayer. Oh, please God, let me hear my night songs soon, with you by my side there, as you are with me here.

Chapter Ten

Abruptly the squawk box boomed an announcement that startled them. "All soldiers are dismissed. Prepare your gear for duty and new orders, and Lt. Sanchez's squad meet us at the communication tent. This area is now off limits to all personnel unless ordered otherwise. Nursing staff to the Mash tents for incoming wounded". Joe and the Sarge looked around for Lt. Sanchez. Their squad was singled out and now they, plus everyone else was off and running. Whatever had been prepared for them before was no longer in their thoughts. Stepping in behind Lt. Sanchez, they took the short cut and were there in less than ten minutes. Lt. Sanchez looked around to make sure all were accounted for. Satisfied, he lifted the tent flap.

It took a few minutes to adjust their eyes to the dimness. Scanning the area they saw the three Captains, the Major and the dog, who was chained to a table leg, next to the busy men and women handling Charts, Maps and Phones. After the Lt. Sanchez spoke to one of the Captains, the Major began to talk. "I don't have time now to mince words and don't intend to. Your squad has to be ready to move out in three days. You will be the only ones to have knowledge and sole use of the weapon we are going to demonstrate.

It's ironic that new orders came in now, or we might have made the same error that has caused the failure before. Whether it will work depends on you. If it can't be utilized as it was intended, it will be destroyed before you leave. This weapon has been a success in practically every war fought. The difficulty has been so far, with us. Now it's up to you and there isn't much time. This mission is top secret".

With that having been said, the Major summoned the Captain who held the familiar whistle in his hand. He stepped forward, walked over to the dog and snapped him to a leash and went into the middle of the squad. He also took a moment to introduce two others that would join the squad if all went well after the three days. Majors' Betty Franconi and Ruth Defore. The Captain said they were highly regarded doctors, an asset where ever they had been stationed.

Continuing, the Captain walked the dog in a circle, occasionally snapping the dog's head up when he became distracted. Slowly he was led, passing each one in the squad. As they approached Joe and the Sergeant, the dog's demeanor changed. He straightened his body, head up, with an ever so slight movement in his tail that looked like a wag. Stopping in front of the two men, the Captain stood facing them. He handed over the dog, along with his leash, to Joe, and stepped back a few feet. The dog sat down on his haunches right by Joe's ankle. Looking toward the Captain then up to Joe's face, he waited, as they all did, for what was to come next.

"This dog is a fighting machine and his jaws can snap a bone like a feather. He knows the difference between our weapons, every kind, and the enemy's. He can sniff out friend or foe by the sweat they emit. He knows what we've taught him, plus an instinct to protect our soldiers. With all the good things I've just told you, he has a massive flaw we had not counted on, and so far cannot correct."

"It's this defect that makes him a liability and not an asset. He's unmanageable, showing no connection or bonding with anyone he's been around, and will not obey without a loud whistle. You all know, behind Enemy lines, silence can mean the difference between life and death. Now his, and your lives, may depend on two men I just handed him over to" the Captain continued, "I realize what I have just said was confusing. We had hoped to put this dog through longer trails, but now with the new Orders, time is of the essence. When we arrived, we came into the mess tent for coffee. I had the dog with me, since he can't be trusted with others. He slipped through his collar and to our surprise and relief, ended up by you, Cpl. Crocker. Not only showing his approval of you, but also protection and obedience. All of this without a whistle or audible sounds."

"His reluctance to leave your side and that of Sergeant Garrity is absolute must for his effectiveness as a top-notch Soldier of trust. It is up to you both now, to take him to the same field we just left, and put him through his paces. Tonight at dusk we begin. You have this time before hand to take him, and see if he will relate to you both. This can't be a guess or wishful thinking."

"You must be a working unit in three days. Your squad and two others are scheduled to go behind enemy lines. They have information that we must have without delay. The perimeter of the field will be closely guarded against anyone else entering. Our original thinking was to let everyone see him work. Now we realize this will definitely fail if word goes beyond "need to know" status. Your entire squad must work as one, dog included."

"I am going to reiterate a point the Major made. You must not make the fate of this dog interfere with the effectiveness with which you all must work together. Sentiment will not save lives. Take him to your quarters, or where ever you think will be beneficial, for the next three hours and then meet me on the north side of the field in full gear. I have further orders for the Doctors, and the three of us will join you at 1700 hours. Dismissed."

Outside the men in the squad were slapping each other on the back. Joe slipped the collar and leash off the dog, letting him jab at his and the Sgt.'s ankles. He ran around in circles yapping and jumping up on each member of the squad, finally settling down to jog closely beside Joe. The Sergeant and Joe decided to head back to their tent to hash over what they just heard and where to go from there. As they continued walking silence fell on them all. It was as if the enormity of what was just said and the orders they had been given, sank in. Even the frisky play of the dog ceased and he fell in stride with them.

"Behind enemy lines!" "Information needed to save "lives"! "Three days"! Joe was deep in thought. They had been there before, many times, but something about the way the Major said it, was more foreboding than Joe could remember. When he was given the leash and the brown eyes looked up at him, it brought him the needed joy, missing in his life. Now his sadness hit him hard; as this beautiful creature was the much talked about "secret weapon".

How foolish to make believe, in this place and time, he would be given an animal to love and want to take home. This was a little boys dream in an adult mind. The Sgt.'s voice broke into his thoughts. "What about Fella for the dog's name. It can be spoken softly, even at night, outside, without any give away echo. He deserves better, but it's too late now". Repeating the name out loud several times in the dogs direction, brought an immediate response from him.

The dog was jumping up and down as each one of the squad called him, "Fella". It was something he didn't have before, a friendly touch instead of a jerk of his neck, and a pat on his head of caring. Joe thought again, "It's not too late for love, my Fella. Not yet."

Chapter Eleven

The men picked up their pace. Catching up to them, the huffing and puffing mail clerk handed them their mail. The Sarge's mail was already in its own sack; so dispensing it didn't take much time. The men stuffed their letters in their coats and continued on. Passing the mess hall they realized they had not eaten.

Going inside their own tent, they were surprised to find hot coffee and sandwiches. The news must be all over the camp, that tonight was important to everyone, not just one particular squad. The men ate and drank hurriedly. Even Fella had been left some dog food, which he ate with gusto.

Checking and re-checking their gear didn't take long. They had been preparing for new orders for some time, knowing each day or hour they could be on the move. As they methodically went through things, Fella went to each one sniffing various scents. Sometimes getting in their way, Joe or Sarge would give a sound or a wave that Fella seemed to understand.

They didn't need to verbally command him, which one of the men commented on to Joe. It was then that Joe realized he and Sarge, unconsciously were using the night songs from home to instruct Fella, and he was catching on. This "special" language they used between the two of them, without thinking or planning. It was this communication that had saved the squad's lives many times, the same talk the men tried to learn but couldn't.

Placing their mail under their pillow and putting their Bibles inside their shirts, Joe and the Sergeant took Fella outside to work with him while the rest of the men finished up. It would be a silent basic training that they had agreed upon. Before beginning, the two had prayer. This, along with their Bibles, was not unusual for them. They had never begun or finished a mission without doing it. It was a part of "gearing up" that the entire squad did.

They all had received a verbal reprimand for doing this, but thankfully it was not a direct command of "cease and desist", which they wouldn't have disobeyed. Not one man would put anyone else's' life in danger just for their own private need. They realized the heavy load they had to carry on their bodies, and the decision for each, was separate and private. No one stopped doing what they thought was right. For their own inner peace, and being close to God. Their gear stayed as intact as did the respect they had for each other.

Sprinting away as far as they could from distractions, the next hour and a half of commands and instructions left all three lying on the ground exhausted. Fella was superbly trained in warfare before coming to them, and any doubt they had, was erased by his stamina and performance. His distant aloof behavior prior to joining Joe was gone. He was one of them now. Not by snapping a chain around his throat, but by a loving arm around his neck. Fella crawled over to where Joe was resting on his back. He put his head softly on Joe's chest, brown eyes looking up at him. Joe reached over and began stroking him, crooning a soft night song.

They had a little time yet before the big test. The final test, and one that would decide if Fella went with them or stayed behind. Behind to a fate Joe didn't want to think about right now. He just wanted Fella to feel all the love that went from his heart into the hand touching him. As Joe opened his eyes after a brief rest, Fella stood up, sensing the approach of the rest of the squad. They joined, complete as a unit, ready to go.

As they approached the field, the Major and the Doctors were already waiting there for them. The Sgt. asked permission to have five minutes to take Fella, with the two new members of their squad, off to the side. Permission was granted. The Sergeant had Fella sniff their gear, clothes and bodies. He explained to them that the dog needed to know the scent of the women, a distinct advantage out in the field. He also had them touch and stroke Fella making a sound that he taught only them That sound, along with others he would teach them later, would be necessary for their mission and survival.

As they circumvented the entire field, the squad encountered what they had gone through previously in real battle situations. Gunfire, grenades, land mines and booby traps, each handled with stealth, courage and wisdom.

They all worked as a team and Fella was both outstanding and tireless. He had an uncanny instinct to drop on his stomach, crawl to a "live" buried mine, and freeze. Joe would then do the same and disarm it. When something came up, Fella went to whom ever needed assistance. Often Fella knew, before hand, and just went to the very spot of trouble.

As they finished cleaning and checking the entire area, they approached the group of Native Villagers so silently, they surrounded them in an instant. They were apparently "friendly "and not the Enemy. They welcomed the squad in their own language, mingled with some English. They offered to share their sparse meal and warm evening fire. With respectful smiles and nods, the Sgt's team searched each one, weapons never lowering, and always on full alert. Doctors Franconi and Defore, given the "go-ahead", checked their bandages to make sure the wounds were real and not used for hidden weapons of any kind.

Satisfied of their search, the Sergeant accepted their offer and also began to give out some of their rations plus a few clean bandages and medicine to them. This was often done in battle. It enabled both sides to learn a little of each other's Language, and customs, to possibly remember faces they might encounter at a later time.

Fella, along with two men, stayed back, keeping alert for any surprises. Fella seemed agitated and restless. He paced from the outskirts, back to Joe, then around the villagers. This didn't go unnoticed by Joe or the Sergeant, and the next instant, Fella attacked a man of the village. He took him down, by the throat, teeth buried in his neck, drawing blood.

Bouncing to Fella's side, Sarge held a gun at the man's temple, saying in his Native Tongue "don't move". Joe, working from the bottom of the feet, even felt the folds of the man's clothing. Coming to a bandaged, padded, bloodied elbow, Joe carefully put a gentle amount of pressure on the lump of padding. The area had an abnormal hard lump in it. Major Defore whispered he might bleed to death but Joe silenced the Doctor with a glance.

Villagers included. Working quickly, he removed the He took a knife and carefully slit the bandage, keeping his hand on the hard lump. It was a grenade and he could see only the bottom of it. The squad cleared the area, rest of the cloth from around the grenade. The pin was still in the grenade. Finally taking a breath, he took it and put it in his jacket pocket. Joe put his hand on Fella's head. Fella's jaws let go, but his face was still next to the Man's throat, who by now had passed out.

Chapter Twelve

Flood Lights illuminated the entire field almost blinding the men. From outside the area the Major's voice broke the silence by asking if it was secure for entry. Given the "permission" to approach, the medical team hurried to the downed man. Joe's squad, including Fella, formed up mulling over the preceding events. Although it was a cool night, they were covered in sweat. They had much to discuss, but the Major and two Captains were already amongst them. Coming to a full attention, they waited, expecting to be reprimanded for the injury to the villager.

Upon asking them if they were all right, the Major began to speak. "You were closely observed and monitored from the beginning. Your performance as a unit is first rate. The dog's reaction was outstanding. We will keep you informed of injured man and his condition. He volunteered his role and knew the possible consequences. Had his death been imminent, sharp shooters would have prevented it". "Lt. Sanchez, dismiss your squad. You will join me now to continue preparation and instructions concerning the mission. You have all done a fine job. There are some rough spots I expect you to work out. Dismissed."

Lt. Sanchez asked to speak to the Sergeant and Joe. The Sergeant had asked both Doctors to come back to their tent, to bring all their gear and belongings. That as a totally well knit Unit, they needed to work, and live, together. The success of the job they needed to do would only work by a cohesive conscious effort.

They were told, if they had any objections, to state them now. None was given. With a final check of the surroundings, they gathered their gear. Departing for their tent, two more had been added to their squad. They had entered that field confident of their ability to work together, like-minded. There could be no doubts now. Two days to knit tight each move, thought and action. They had their work cut out, but by their strides as they departed, there was no indication this group of soldiers had any concept of failure. They all had pure, honest determination for saving lives, and for serving their Country, to the very best of their abilities, even unto death.

Two of the men were sent to procure some chow and bring it to them while they settled in for the night. It was late but along with hunger, adrenalin was surging through their veins. Sleep for now wasn't given any thought. Fella entered first, bouncing from bunk to bunk, checking each one as they came in. Hands reached out patting, hugging and stroking him. Joe never made it all the way in the tent opening. Fella hit him chest high, and both went down amidst shouts and laughter.

The food and the Doctors arrived at the same time, bringing more release from the tension of the previous hours. Although they weren't sure what they were eating, it tasted good, even the coffee. Fella consumed his in record time, and sensing this momentary release from tension, his eyes checked with Joe, for approval, before eating anything other than his own. Right here in this moment, mistakes, misunderstandings, and what had happened before, was put on hold. They needed the "now". Joe nodded to Fella, who immediately jumped on every one of the guy's laps, devouring any little scrap of dropped food. Fella had a family, filled with love freely given to him, which he gave back. Plunking down by Joe, from his head to his foot, their hearts were entwined, forever.

Lt. Sanchez's de-briefing lasted for several hours. He passed on many orders from the Major. One of significance was that Fella was to be trained to carry a neck pouch. Although transmissions of information were usually accurate from the front lines back to headquarters, the need for absolute silence was imperative for this mission. Maps, Fuel Depots, Troop Strength, and Weapon Capability, all of this particular Information, had to be sent back, at utmost speed. Fella was to carry these statistics in the pouch, for as many trips as necessary. He would also have to help to get the squad as close as possible, without detection, and safely back.

The land was highly mined. That was Fella's expertise. Whatever mine he encountered, he drew attention to it, to be defused. Headquarters felt the reason Fella could not be handled was for a special reason. A Mine, that he had found, detonated, resulting in the loss of a soldier. Fella had gone on ahead and wasn't physically hurt. The Military Veterinarian determined it was so traumatic that he had shut down to relationships, the same as a Human would go into "shell shock".

Had he not "bonded" with Joe, he was scheduled to be "Put Down'. His knowledge was as a soldier, not as a pet. His usefulness was gone, until that day. Joe listened, not realizing Fella had come next to him on the bunk. Joe had automatically put his arm around Fella's neck. Joe was thankful for whatever time they would have together. The rest of the de-briefing was pretty clear-cut. Lt. Sanchez turned to the Major Defore's direction, and re-iterated the fact that getting the information back, was to save the lives of many, not just one. That the wounded, that needed to be treated, would be returned, "after" obtaining the objective. Lt. Sanchez excused himself. They would begin again at zero five hundred.

With most of them sacked out, Joe reached under his pillow to read the letters from Pa and Sara. He was tired but needed to connect with them. The news was good. Pa felt healthy, fishing every day, when he wasn't obeying Sara's orders on what needed fixing. Sharing meals at the shack or with her family was getting to be a routine for them all. He told Joe, that he was so "far ahead" of Daniel, in the checker game, it was "pitiful". If he had all the money they had pretend betting, he would be living "high on the hog", Joe had to laugh out loud at that.

Sara had sent a picture of her and Pa fishing in the dugout. Pa had aged quite a bit but his face said it all. Happy!!!! This one was in color and Joe could see her hair shining from the sun's rays, her smile was lovely. She was sitting down, holding a big bass up, for all to see. Joe wanted to make sure he wrote both of them before he left. He couldn't tell them where he was or going. Their letters came to a special mail depot in his name.

His longing for home was deeply felt. Missing the night songs and what they meant to him. Perhaps he and everyone could go back to their loved ones. Soon, this conflict would end. He would write them tomorrow. He wanted them both to know he loved them. Joe suddenly realized he had not used that word to Sara before. He tried to think if it was really so, or because he was home sick. Patting a sleeping Fella on the head, he grinned. He meant it. He loved Sara. He was more frightened of that right now than what was ahead. He would say it in his letter. It was important for her to know, especially now. As tired as Joe was before, he couldn't sleep. Getting up from his knees, and sliding into his bunk, he didn't see Fella watching him, as he said his prayers.

Chapter Thirteen

They were almost to the front lines. It had been a grueling few days with little sleep. Joe heard the wounded Villager was doing well. He required several stitches but was up and around. The words of the Major, on the field during exercises stuck in Joe's mind. "Had his death been eminent, a sharp shooter would have prevented it". Joe shivered because he knew it meant Fella would have been shot.

Each one had written letters and posted them. Joe said what was in his heart to Sara. He asked Pa to watch over her until he returned. Telling him he loved them both. He wondered what Pa would write back and say about that. He was anxious to get a letter from Sara too. Suppose she didn't feel the same or there was someone else in her life. There were many questions but no answers, at least not for now. Joe had noticed the Sarge and Major Defore had hit it off really well. So well in fact, they spent not only training time together, but now were inseparable. He hadn't said anything to the Sargent. Teasing was well in order, but maybe later.

The sound of gunfire and mortar shells brought Joe from his quiet thinking. Quickly they joined up with three other squads that had arrived earlier. They had their orders, and they got down to War business. It would be Night -Time in an hour. The earlier rain had subsided and a slice of moonlight appeared. It would be just right for them to proceed on foot, high lighting enough, but not so much, as to give them away. It was a mile from the line that they were holding. Most of the men had dug in here at first, leaving gear that was not needed for the moment. Essentials went on their backs, waists and shoulders. Pockets were filled. Fella had his "gear" put on him. His muscles were tense but he was calm, following Joe.

Joe took Fella to the communication officer. He was one that Fella would deliver the messages to. Joe made sure that he got his scent plus those around him. If the officer went "down", Joe wanted Fella to know just who else to go to. He was greeted silently but with a "hands on" meeting. Sniffing each one would make it easier for Fella to differentiate only those that would handle the pouches. One was to deliver and one was to take back to Joe, the Sergeant or Lt. Sanchez.

Fella learned before leaving training camp, that those three would be his contacts. Joe knew it also meant if one was hit, he would be able to continue the transfers with no interruption.   The messages were in code. Should anyone be captured, the contents couldn't be forced out of them, because, they couldn't decipher it. If Fella was unable to deliver, other measures had already been arranged. It was imperative, that facts of this particular stronghold were known.

To secure this area meant being nearer to the finish of this long conflict, a conflict that had taken an immense toll on so many lives. Lt. Sanchez motioned them to move out. He, along with Joe and Fella took the point. Sergeant Garrity brought up the rear. In single file, they disappeared into the night.

The area ahead was filled with land mines and traps. Joe was the best they had to defuse them. Getting as many now would be less to handle in the morning. Joe knew they would be re checked, so he was careful not to disturb the area around them, alerting the opposite side of their presence. He checked brush and stubs for trigger wires. Totally in blackness by now, they retreated to base camp to wait for dawn.

Joe hated to retreat because up ahead were a handful of men, dug in, waiting for them. They had been there three days, gathering information. With no fresh contact, they depended on help to come. If they had to cut out suddenly, they wouldn't make it.

After briefing the communication officer, Lt. Sanchez gathered the men around him. They discussed just how they would proceed. They had a Map that showed the location of each man ahead. It was brought back the previous day. Of the three men designated to bring back the information, only one returned.

The field they had used to get there had been laid with fresh mines. Deciding to minimize giving away their location, he came alone and they remained. He told of making his way mostly on his stomach, "feeling" every foot ahead. He was sure they wouldn't move unless forced to. Not hearing any sudden or hurried gunfire since returning, he was pretty sure the map was accurate.

Eating their cold K-rations, Joe whispered, "Hey Sarge, I sure could use a cup of that hot oily coffee", what about you?" The Sergeant nodded in the affirmative. Thin blankets couldn't keep the cold out of their bones. Joe missed Fella lying beside him.

After settling down, Fella had returned about a hundred feet toward the front. He was on guard, his previous action kicking in. He was trained as a Soldier first, and only upon direct command would he have left his post. Joe couldn't see him but felt his presence. As they prayed together that night, Joe also sent his love out to Fella's direction. "Someday boy, we'll hear those night songs together and all of this will be left behind, you'll be safe".

Majors Franconi and Defore went to the temporary First Aid tent to minister to wounded and re-pack the supplies they would need. One of them accompanied Lt. Sanchez and his men. They would decide themselves based upon their actual combat experience plus types of injuries that were present. Major Franconi was the one that came back to the squad. Laying her gear beside her, she slipped under her blanket, there wasn't much time before daybreak, and weariness was upon her, as it was with the men. Looking around, she noticed Fella wasn't there. Motioning that observance to Joe, who was still awake, she gave a night song sound signifying that question, and he pointed to where he was, darkness obliterating any sign of him. Thumbs up between them seemed to reconfirm joined admiration.

They carefully traveled the path they had been down before; each one double-checking previous mines, plus new ones that had been set. Quietly reaching each foxhole, they found the messages that were slipped into Fella's pouch and he was sent back. He made three round trips in the first two hours they were there. He wasn't given much time to rest in between trips. A quick drink of water, a hug from Joe, the pouch filled and then emptied.

Checking his watch, Fella had not returned and too much time had gone by. Joe wasn't alarmed exactly, just the anticipation of his return. He knew some messages would take longer to de-code. He and the others were using binoculars, making metal notes of what they saw. Any information they could take back would be valuable. What was keeping Fella?

Motioning to the Sergeant, Joe was all set to go after him. Catching on, Lt. Sanchez's face dismissed that idea, and his displeasure was evident.

Coming in on his stomach, there was blood on Fella's leg, and there was no telling what else was behind them now. It appeared to be a small cut on the pad of one foot. The Lt. indicated a wait and hold position. The order was silently given, "information sufficient, CUT OUT, CUT OUT, CUT OUT."

Slipping quietly but with urgency, the foxholes were emptied. They were in small groups, men taking the point checking for mines. Those that were left bring up the rear, were re-checking each step. No time now to be complaisant. Up ahead they could see that a small, hand-to-hand battle had taken place. Still forms were lying on the ground, the eerie peacefulness of death. Joe sensed that Fella had chosen to bypass this instead of fighting. He must have known to take that final pouch to those up ahead.

Major Franconi paused long enough to feel for pulses. Finding a viable one, she lifted the man upon her back, and carried him toward safety. Joe counted eight down that he could see. There was no telling how many more. She was struggling with the extra weight. A big man to carry, she gave no indication of slowing down or quitting. Staying low and continuing to move, some hands reached up to shift him to another back. None of the fallen soldiers would be left behind and going back for them would happen as soon as possible. Counting but seeing no more, they moved rapidly, sensing the approach of opposing forces behind them.

Fella was between the Sergeant and Joe, moving constantly back and forth. He paused at a mine missed by Joe. Alerted by a specific sound of a night song signal, he stopped short, feeling ahead with his knife, and disarmed it. Glancing at Joe, he reached out to Fella with a swift pat. There was only about a half hour until dark and No moon was visible. This was not good, it was taking entirely too long to get back. They, clearly, had been out-smarted. Their position was evidently known, and they were about to be pinned between the two and wiped out. It would have been successful had not their own men followed Fella back with the final instructions.

Help had been coming to them but at a tremendous sacrifice of lost lives. They didn't have much further to go, and the mortars and gunfire were beginning to go off behind them. The signal had gone out, "Fire on the enemy once it was clear they were headed to safety." The Sergeant was off to Joe's left. Fella was about three feet in the front of them, his nose down, sniffing for any more surprises. The sharp point of Joe's knife "felt" the hard object. He disarmed it rapidly.

Hearing a signal from the Sergeant, Joe glanced back to see him laying absolutely still, his hand pointing to his leg. Sliding back over already covered ground, Joe was along side of the Sergeant.

Looking at his leg, he could see the lace of his boot caught on a wire. It was a trip-wire.

Tricky spot, hung tight. Cutting the laces back and forth, from top then to the bottom, like a puzzle. Joe's eyes stung from the salt in his sweat. No time to wipe them. Both hands weaving gingerly, sliding the laces loose enough for the Sergeant to slip his foot out of the boot. Almost happening in slow motion, until he was free and clear.

Relief flashed between them. Fella had stood his ground without moving. He too could feel the tension released. His big droopy tongue hung down, drips of saliva hitting the dirt. The Sergeant moved ahead on his stomach, Joe and Fella right behind him. Pausing for just a moment, Joe took his sleeve and wiped his face. Reaching up to give Fella a hug, his knee bent almost to a half stand. The sound of a soft click, the weight of Fella on his chest, all at the same time, as the explosion went off

Darkness, total darkness, and Joe could only make out garbled sounds. He could detect a word or two, but nothing was making sense. Fluttering his eyes, Joe heard his name being called. Drifting in and out, noises reached out at him. "Let me sleep" his mind kept saying, "Get away from me". Once in awhile he felt this terrible pain but couldn't connect it to any one area.

He heard his name called again. After a struggle, he opened his eyes, blinking to clear away the haziness. Then he saw Sarge's face. Starting to speak, Joe was very unnerved and his throat was incredibly dry like it was full of cotton. A straw slipped through his lips, cool water soon soothed his parched vocal cords. What was the matter with Sarge? Tears were falling down his face, and he looked a wreck. He was unshaven, his uniform, dirty and wrinkled, and he had shaky hands. Something had happened but Joe's mind wouldn't work. He reached out his hand to the Sergeant, but tubes and bandages held it firmly to his side.

Moving his head around a little, Joe recognized he was in some sort of white tent, flat on his back in bed, and again the Sergeant was speaking his name. "Joe, can you hear me? Do you know who I am? It's me, Sarge. Stay with me buddy". Clearing his throat, Joe said, "I'm here, you look and smell terrible. Too lazy to clean up?" As a smile started to appear on the Sgt's face, Joe was hit with nauseating pain. He heard himself scram, then felt a soft sense of drifting back into darkness.

Joe awakened, surprisingly refreshed and alert. He knew he had been hurt. A look around the tent and his white gown confirmed that much. His chest hurt like the dickens. More though, his left leg was throbbing and wouldn't quit. He called out for the Sergeant. He needed someone who would stop and talk to him. He looked down toward his left leg, the site of all the pain. There was a slight dip in the blanket covering the lower part of his legs. Struggling, he lifted the leg. The blanket lifted up slightly, it hurt but seemed to be working just fine. Joe started to remember bits and pieces; almost getting back, seeing the Sgt's boot slip off, hearing the mortar fire. It just wouldn't come to him.

A nurse appeared, wearing a wonderful smile. She gave Joe some more water, checked his tube in his arm, and washed his face with a nice hot cloth. Thanking her, he asked for Sergeant Garrity, and if it wasn't too much trouble, a good cup of hot coffee.

She told him he was just coming in and coffee was on the way. He noticed that Sarge looked better but wondered if he had been hurt too. All his questions would be answered now, and missing pieces would be cleared up.

Why couldn't he remember? Smiling, Joe called out his name, "Sarge, it's about time you showed up. Where's Fella, bring him to me, will you? I need to see him and have him up on this bunk. I will heal a lot quicker singing night songs to him.

It will calm him down also".

Pulling up a chair, Sarge softly said, "I can't do that Joe, we need to talk first". Thinking for a minute, Joe said, "I guess they won't let a dog in here, Germs and all that. I don't hurt too much, so help me up and walk me over to the door. At least he and I can see each other and maybe a quick hug. They won't mind and if they do, who cares, right?" Sarge told Joe that he had been hurt pretty. His left leg in particular, that the Doctors didn't want him up just yet, maybe in a few days.

Chapter Fourteen

They were interrupted by the presence of a man, who said he was Dr. Hudson, and the same nurse, who introduced herself as Abby Shuman. Joe could tell by their Insignia's, they were also Military. The Sergeant stood at attention, but a hand on his shoulder gave him permission to sit again. The Doctor explained they were going to check his injuries and change some bandages.

They removed a lot of cotton padding from Joe's chest area, asking him he if hurt in that area. Joe said it wasn't too bad and asked what had happened. The Doctor described two broken ribs, and severe bruising of his sternum in the heart area. He told Joe his Bible had taken a direct hit; and a long shard of metal had gone into the middle of it, being slowed by the cover and pages, stopping it from going right to his heart. In time they would heal. His face and arms were "chunked" up a bit, no long-term injuries.

Replacing the bandages took quite some time to do, and Joe was visibly pale from the movement and pain. The Doctor glanced at the Sergeant who, for some reason, shook his head silently, indicating a "NO". The Doctor then told Joe to rest, that they would return in a little while to finish up. The Sergeant asked permission to walk with them, and left after telling Joe he was going to grab something to eat. He could tell they were in deep discussion.

It was just as well, because he was suddenly very tired and wanted to sleep. Thinking about what the doctor told him about his Bible, Joe Prayed a humble "Thank You".

His mind was still trying to bring him to the place where it happened. He recalled hearing and reading, that in times of trauma, memory loss was not unexpected. Almost asleep, he knew that Sarge would tell him all about it. He drifted off thinking of Fella. It will be so wonderful to see his big brown eyes and tail going a mile a minute. Joe knew that with Sarge, Fella wouldn't be too lonely and he would soon be up and around to take care of him. He smiled peacefully.

During their talk, the doctor wanted to go back and talk with Joe about his other injuries, but the Sergeant persuaded the doctor to leave them alone for a while after Joe woke up. Getting permission to call home, he spoke to Sara. He didn't have to wait long to get through even with the time difference. She assured him her heart was with him, being thankful that he wasn't that he wasn't hurt also. She said she would go immediately over to Joe's Pa and tell him about the news of Joe. Also that letters to both of them had been mailed the day before. The Sergeant explained to Sara, that Joe would need lots of care when he returned home. Without a pause in her voice, she declared her feeling of love for Joe, asking her brother to relay that to Joe.

Sarge went to the Chapel. He bowed in prayer and asked for help. Joe was like a brother to him, more than a friend. He kneeled awhile, waiting for answers for some of the questions. Speaking humbly to God, he said, "I can't do this by myself, please give me the strength and wisdom to know what to do and say". Into his hear came these words, "My Grace Is Sufficient For You, For My Strength Is Made Perfect In Weakness". Getting up from his knees, he was weary in his body but refreshed in his soul. He still had Joe's Bible in his hands. Turning the pages, he came to the spot where the shard of shrapnel had stopped. Tears streamed down his face, the answer was there. Could he speak the right words of healing comfort? Knowing he was not alone anymore, Sarge made his way back to Joe's bedside.

What in the world was the noise? Joe was deep in sleep until this sound hit his ears. The sounds were like the swamp, when Pa had to clear a tree limb out of the way. "That is what it is, a broken chain saw. I'm at the shack with Pa." Opening his eyes, Joe was looking at the white ceiling. Still hearing that sound, it took him a moment to orientate himself. Looking down to where the noise was coming from, he saw Sarge laying with his head on the foot of the bed. He was asleep and snoring up a storm. Laughing out-loud, he woke up the Sergeant, who nearly fell off his chair. "Boy, for a minute I thought I was at the swamp; and you look just like you crawled out of one".

The pain hit his leg making him grab hold of the sheet. Sarge slid up next to Joe on the bed. Wiping his face, he waited until he seen Joe's hands relax a little. "Joe, we have to talk before the doctor comes back. There are some things I have to tell you about what happened to you on that day". Joe nodded his head "yes," he was ready to hear it all.

"Do you remember anything of what happened?" Getting no response, Sarge continued, "I was up ahead of you and I looked back to see you on one knee, holding Fella around his neck. The next second, the mine went off, before I had time to get to you, to get you out of the way. Are you still with me Joe, or do you want me to quit talking for awhile?" Joe asked for a drink of water, his throat hurt. "Go ahead, I have to hear the rest, please tell me". Sarge continued. "You took a hard hit, my friend. So hard, that your leg was shattered. I want you to know they did everything that was possible to repair the damage. Joe, They had to remove the bottom of your leg, below the knee, they did their very best to save it, but couldn't". Staring at Sarge, Joe said, "that can't be, I feel it. It's there, that's why I am in so much pain. Look, I can lift it up too; there is some mistake. You look under the sheet, you'll see. It's there, I'm telling you".

Gulping for air, Sarge continued. "I was there, I'm telling you". I carried you to the first aid station and they transferred you here. I haven't left your side for the past five days. I wanted to tell you myself instead of the doctors". "The pain you feel is called "Phantom Pain" Joe. The doctors explained it to me. The nerves hurt like the whole leg is there. The pain is real and horrible. I wouldn't lie to you. I prayed that the wounds weren't so severe, but, it couldn't be helped Joe, it's really gone".

After a few minutes of silence, Joe took the Sgt's hand, "I think I can live with this Mark", using the Sgt's name for the first time. "I have to tell Pa and Sara. You don't know, but I love your sister. I wrote and told her in my last letter. They have to know. Oh God, Mark: How can I break this to her now, this changes everything. She will want a "whole man", someone who can take care of her. This will change everything for the both of us".

Still holding Joe's hand, Sarge began to talk again. "I have already called them for you. They both know and ask me to tell you how much you are loved. You will be going home soon, they will both be waiting. She won't notice that your leg gone, and I'm sure that it won't matter. You have to trust me when I tell you this. Sara looks into the heart, not at how a person walks or talks. She is very special, that's why you fell in love with her so deeply without even meeting her".

Chapter Fifteen

Seeing the doctor approaching, Sarge got up from the bed and sat back down in his chair. "Listen Joe, they're coming back now to finish changing your bandages. I'm sure they will also want to explain things to you. Are you alright?" Joe was quiet. His face was covered in sweat from the pain of his wounds on his body, and from the pain in his heart for Pa and Sara. He shook his head, indicating that he was managing for now.

After they arrived, the Sergeant took the doctor aside, and told him that he had filled Joe in on what has had happened to him. Before they started, the nurse asked Joe if he was going to be all right and if wanted to see the Chaplain when they were finished. Continuing the conversation and without waiting for an answer, the doctor relayed to him that in a week or so, as soon as they could stabilized him, he was going back stateside.

He wouldn't go directly home, but to a hospital to finish healing and for rehabilitation. So he could learn about prosthetic devices to help him walk again. Joe listened without saying a word. His face was pale and drawn. So much had been thrown at him all at once. He began to shake and shiver. Waves of nausea started to double him up, causing him to groan with pain. The doctor shouted orders to the staff. "He's going into shock. Let's get moving here".

Sarge was shoved out of the way. Tubes, IV's, blankets, trays of medication and bandages now surrounded the bed. Seeing the look of fear on the Sgt's face, nurse Shuman took his arm. She comforted him as best as she could, and explained that this sometimes happens. Often shock could be delayed, and then hit a person really hard. The main thing was to take his vitals, bringing them as close to normal as possible. That shock could be life threatening if not taken care of immediately.

She directed Sarge to a chair in the hall, assuring him she would come back for him soon. Looking at his watch, Sarge saw that it had been two hours. Getting up, he began to pace back and forth. Finally nurse Shuman was walking toward him. "He's doing better now, we gave him a pretty heavy sedative and he should sleep for about four hours or more.

Why don't you go to the Temporary Housing? I'll phone ahead for you, get you a room, so you can change your clothes. Take a nice hot shower and eat a good meal. You don't look so good yourself right now. Sleep if you can. Joe's is going to need you until we ship him out. By the way, he keeps mumbling about night songs and somebody named Fella. If he is with you, it might be a good idea to bring this guy with you later. Joe needs his buddies around him right now".

Sarge's head dropped into his hands, tears streaming down his face. Nurse Shuman put her arms around him, and she began to rock him like a child. "It's alright, we're going to do our best for him here, have Faith, don't give up. He's young and strong but it will take time. Sarge told her about home, night songs and Fella. They stood up and with a hug, she sent him off to rest. Sarge stopped at the Chapel, giving humble Thanks for Joe being alive and asking for strength and guidance.

At the office of temporary housing, Sarge asked where the pay phones were. He needed to talk to Major Defore. Getting directions and some change, he was relieved hear her voice. They talked for almost an hour. She said she would let the squad, and all of them there, about Joe's condition. She was worried about him and he assured her he was going to take care of himself that he would be back with her in a few days. He really wanted them to take some time, if they could get it and talk. Hanging up, he headed for his room.

Walking down the corridor it was fairly quiet. Getting into bed, he fell asleep almost immediately. Waking up with a start, it took him a minute or so to remember where he was. Looking at his watch, he had slept longer than he had planned. He was worried that Joe had awakened and not seeing him, would be frightened or feel alone. In his heart he prayed that he was still sleeping. The last few hours was enough to exhaust him; what was Joe going through?

Going into Joe's room, Sarge could see his eyes still closed. Lifting a chair, he sat down as still as he could, trying not to disturb him. He had carried Joe's Bible with him all this time because he wanted to make sure it wouldn't get lost. Not tonight, not now.

Putting It next to his heart, Sarge silently went through Verses he remembered as a child and now as a grown man. Glancing up at Joe, he was startled to see his eyes watching him. "I'm sorry Joe, I wanted you to sleep and get some strength back. You had a really bad time a little while ago. You don't have to talk, we just can be here together and you feel free to doze off, OK?

Joe smiled at him, "Thank you for coming back and being with me. I know you are tired and I'm sorry to be such a burden. You have suffered right along with me Mark. I have been so selfish not to have noticed. I especially thank you for being the one to tell me about my leg. It would have been so cold to have a stranger drop that kind of news on me. How are you doing or have you had a chance to catch your breath? I've taken all of your time and I ask your Forgiveness.

Is everyone in the squad all right? I have been so into myself I never even asked. You are my friend, like my brother, and I didn't take the time to make sure you weren't hurt".

The kindness and love shown to Sarge over whelmed him. Here was a man who had lost his leg and almost his life, asking Him if he was all right. He reached up and took Joe's hand in his. Neither spoke for a few minutes. "We all made it fine, Joe. I talked to Major Defore earlier; everyone has been praying for you and sends their love".

Joe nodded. "I really need to see Fella. It's important for him to be with me. You know he came to us in a bad way. He had no one who really loved him before us. I know he's a part of you too. With the three of us being together, it will put his mind at rest, taking the bad memories away, and giving him peace. That at last and forever he has us. I know I'm going back stateside, and the Army won't let me take him with me, anyway not now. He can be a big help right here, you have seen that for yourself. We would never have made it back safely without him. There's no telling what the next few months, or even years, have in store for him. He will be with you and then you both can come home together.

I have to admit that losing my leg has me scared. I have told you that I love Sara, and you've assured me it won't matter to her. It might though, Mark. You've known her a lot longer than me. Sometimes, a person will stay, in a situation,, out of kindness, putting aside their own real feelings.

Soon I'll be leaving this terrible place, and I'll be leaving you and also Fella. I am comforted that you will be together. The truth is, I'm not really handling things well. They have me on some pretty stiff pain medication. It helps the physical part of me, but I have sorrow in my heart, and I don't understand it all yet".

16
Chapter Sixteen

Chapter Sixteen

Joe paused, taking a breath. The sweat was again on his brow. Sarge took a wet warm cloth and tenderly wiped his face. He asked him if he needed some medication and if he needed to sleep for a little while. He reminded him that his body was suffering shock and needed rest.

Joe declined. Thanking him for his concern. "I really want to talk tonight. Tomorrow will be a busy day for me. It's right we do this now. No one is interrupting us. The two men other men in the room are sleeping. They've had a bad day also. If you aren't too tired, I would like to continue.

At first, when you told me about losing my leg, I wanted to scream at God. I was so filled with rage. Off and on today, I have been praying for forgiveness. I have my life. A life filled with happiness, given more blessings than I deserve. We've seen this country, so torn apart. People are fighting for something that has no true meaning; for territory and dominance, resulting in cruelty, bloodshed and immense sorrow. When it's all over, then what? In our Country, dead and wounded and in this Country, dead and wounded. Nothing really will be settled. All is in vain.

Only God knows this world He Created. We must live by His Grace, the way He would have us live. The important thing for us is to trust and have Faith in Him. We should remember that we are not alone, if we keep Him above all other things. Mark, I want you to be careful here, to come home to us. I know I have taken up a lot of your time talking. I have said what was in my heat and would like to hear your feelings also, if you don't mind".

"Joe, I'm humbled that you can talk with me. I can't pretend to understand what you are feeling. I don't know, given the same circumstance, if I could say or act the way you do. I tried to imagine that it was me, and just that thought, filled me with so many emotions I had to stop. I will be so thankful when this is over. Seems every ten or fifteen years another war breaks out and the cycle starts all over again. We know what the Scriptures tell us, and you are right. Faith and trust must sustain us always. If we lose then there is no hope.

I have your Bible with me. I don't know if you remember the doctor telling you about what happened to it". Joe nodded and said he remembered a little. Something about shrapnel hitting it. Getting up and sitting on the bed besides Joe, Sarge showed him the cover. There was a very small hole in the leather. Opening it up, Sarge turned the pages, pointing to the hole, slicing each page and stopping. There was an indentation, a point where it had stopped. "I want to read where it stopped Joe. It will tell you something you have to know".

He began reading: "GREATER LOVE HAS NO ONE THAN THIS, THAN TO LAY DOWN ONE'S LIFE FOR HIS FRIENDS. Do you understand what I'm saying to you Joe?" There was nothing but silence and an empty look on Joe's face. Taking a deep breath, his throat constricting, Sarge went on. "I can't bring Fella to you Joe. He didn't make it. When I got to back to where you were, he was laying on top of you. He took it all Joe. He gave you his life. He didn't have time to feel pain, only his love, which went beyond what you and I can comprehend. We were given this incredible gift from God in giving us Fella. His gift to us will have no measure. I brought him back Joe. He will go home to the states with you. Not in the way we wanted, but he will never be alone again. He was loved, and always will be".

Joe's head snapped back into his pillow. He grabbed his sheets then raised his hands into the air. He was screaming but no sounds were coming out of his mouth. Sarge scooped him up into his arms, holding him like a baby. Streams of tears were falling down both of their faces. No sounds, no words, for two men on a small hospital bed, enveloped in a journey of pain, sorrow, despair and emptiness.

Dawn broke that morning on a scene no one in the hospital would forget. There were two men, sharing the terrible loss of their friend, their buddy, Fella. Only nurse Shuman was aware of what had just happened. She softly came to them. Checking Joe as best as she could for the moment, she lovingly unwound their arms. Laying Joe gently back on his pillow, she wrapped another blanket over him to still his shaking body.

Touching the Sgt's shoulder, she guided him back onto the chair. Kneeling face to face with him, her eyes met his, with a kind understanding. Wiping his face, she whispered to him that the Chaplain was just outside to be with Joe and him. Sarge closed his eyes for a moment to regain control. Speaking softly, he asked her to send the Chaplain in to see Joe. He asked the nurse to please examine his friend Joe again, as he was concerned what this news had done to him. He would wait outside for her to come back.

Coming back to the Sergeant, nurse Shuman pulled up a chair for herself and sat down next to him, visibly shaken. Sarge thought about what she must face each day. Taking care of wounded soldiers, some never leaving here alive, no matter what she did for them. The toll it must take on her and all those other caregivers. He asked her if he could help in some way. She just took his hand thanking him.

The Chaplain was leaving and nurse Shuman had instructions for the Sergeant. "Today and tomorrow will be very exhausting for Joe; we have surgery scheduled later today because the wound on his leg needs some more cleaning up. We have to make sure no infection sets in. When we can send him home, depends on how stable he is. He and the Chaplain just had prayer and Joe was a little more at peace.

He fell asleep a little while ago. I wanted to give him a pain shot but he declined although he did take a small sedative."

"I want you to back to housing. Please take some time for yourself. We would rather you come back tomorrow. You have been given permission to stay until it is time for him to leave. Sorry, but your orders still can change at any minute, it's really heating up on the front. And, unfortunately, you are definitely needed there. Your squad depends on you, and you have to be fit to lead them. You must regain some strength yourself."

"Your permission to accompany Joe, after he was wounded, and staying all this time, speaks how highly regarded you are. Someone will call you there when you can visit again. If I don't get a chance to see you before you leave, it's been an honor to know you. Joe's getting the very best medical attention we can give him, and you gave him your best emotional support. Now we step out of the way and give him to God. Take care, my new friend."

Chapter Seventeen

The abrupt loud knocking at his door woke up the Sergeant. Groggy and trying to get up to answer, he was greeted by a soldier in full dress uniform. "Sorry to wake you like this, but you have orders to return to your squad. You only have about four hours, and there has been some mix up about sending Fella Back with Cpl. Crocker. I'll wait out here for you to gear up. Sorry, but you'll have to eat on the run too. Got some hot grub here, but not much time, and we've a lot to do, sorry Sarge".

Fast was not the word for how he got ready. Half choking, he spilled coffee on his clean boxer shorts. His mind was racing, "What Kind of problem with Fella? I have to get back to see Joe. I just can't leave without saying good-bye to him. Oh please Father, help me to fix things with the time they gave me".

Joe had done well with the surgery but the pain was unbelievable. He couldn't comprehend how a leg, that wasn't there, could still hurt. They had explained to him about "phantom pain", but he knew his ankle was giving him fits, he told them so. He couldn't share the hurt in his heart about Fella, that kind of sorrow could only be shared with Sarge.

He wondered where Sarge was. He did have an appetite and would have liked to have eaten breakfast with him. The tray was loaded with food, real eggs and bacon. The coffee didn't have an oily taste, which made him want more than the two cups they gave him. He had a little trouble with nausea but nothing he couldn't handle.

They were coming in a short time to get him up for the first time. He was nervous about that. He had sat up by himself when no one was looking. It was only leaning forward halfway, but he had orders not to move around too much without help. He smiled, "I am still as stubborn as I used to be. I will have to pray about willfulness and pride, it has been a stumbling block for me".

There were plenty of hands holding him, but along with the pain, he didn't want to pass out. Standing up, even for just a few minutes, brought back the nausea and the throbbing in his leg. His chest didn't bother him much, and he wondered to himself how long it would take to get well again. Back in bed, the bandages were changed along with his Bed Clothes, and he was drenched with sweat from the rapid movements.

Nurse Shuman gave him a bath and shaved him. "There, you look human again, and mighty handsome at that, for a while there we called you the "bearded wonder". You have surprised and amazed us all at how well you are doing, both physically and mentally. Now, you have to be honest with me, Joe. Don't put on a brave front for others. I have to know truthfully. We can see the wounds beginning to heal, but going home depends on what I observe, what the stats on your chart says, and how the Chaplain reports this situation. Do you understand?" Joe said he would never lie to her. He wanted to live; because his Pa was at the swamp waiting for him. He truly knew in his heart, he had been spared for a purpose. Too many had died in this conflict, saving others, his life included. He asked her if she knew about Fella.

Holding her feelings in check, she told Joe that she and the Sergeant had spent a lot of time talking about their beautiful dog. She even knew about the poor soldier laying on his back in the mess tent, Fella ready to chew him to pieces. They both roared with laughter until tears were streaming down both their faces. Catching their breaths, they cried with sadness for Fella, not noticing the other soldiers lying in their bed crying also.

Joe was propped up reading his letters that finally were forwarded to him. Each and every one more endearing than he knew possible. Pa's was filled with hope and pride for him, anticipating his return. Sara, not only expressed her love for him, but she too was happy about him returning home. She told him that legs were just an easy and lazy way to get around. That made him smile. Her letter was filled with all the plans she had made for them to go fishing, have picnics and take long walks in the twilight, listening to night songs. She said she didn't want to appear forward, that it was up to him if he wanted to be with her. He could tell, and read between the lines, the sweetness of her heart.

All of a sudden the sound of loud running footsteps filled the air. Bursting through the door, Sarge slipped on puddle of water, and slid belly down, right past Joe's bed and into the wall. Laughter filled the ward. Sarge sat upright, helmet encasing his face so that all they could see was hair sticking up, surrounding a head without eyes, nose or mouth. Prying it off, there he sat, with an audience clapping and cheering, yelling 'safe, score one for our team'.

With a sheepish grin, he got back on his feet and went over to Joe. Seeing the looks of bewilderment, he spoke so quickly that Joe held up his hand to slow down, take a breath". "Sorry friend, don't have much time. I am heading back to the squad. Got my orders this morning. You O.K.?" Getting a nod yes, he went on. "I thought I would be able to see you off to the hospital from the airport, but the Army made other plans for me.

When you get to the plane, Fella will be there waiting. No matter what you hear, or what's said to you, go along with it. Say as little as possible. You will be going back together. Trust me Joe, It's all arranged. Do exactly as I told you.

There's so much I want to say. I'm proud of you, and having you as my brother, my friend, is truly a gift from God. I couldn't have made it without you besides me. I will make it home also Joe. Pray for all of us. Pray this will all be over soon.

You being home and well again will keep me going. I have to go now, there's just no more time here for us. I'll write you when I can. Give my love to everyone at home. Get well now do you hear me? We have a lot to do when I get back. I have a secret fishing hole with catfish so big, it will take two of us, to get just one of them in the boat. I never told you that before, I didn't want to give away all my secrets and have you show me up. Just remember to do what I said at the plane, O.K.?

Joe barely had time to comment on the new stripe on Sarge's uniform. Pointing to it, Sarge mumbled something about a Battle Field promotion. They prayed together, and everyone in the ward bowed their heads also. A fast handshake, an unashamed bear hug and Sarge was gone.

Sarge was going back to the war without Joe watching over him. He laid his head back on the pillow; his emotions were washing over his mind and heart. He was wondering what he meant about Fella and the plane. Joe was awash with fear again. He had buried those feelings for a little while and now they were back. He had been having flashbacks, and counseling was a big help but they would come upon him without warning. He had difficulty controlling the sweating and shaking. The news about Fella had hit him hard, first his death, and now the uncertainty of what would happen to his remains.

Nurse Shuman came, wiped his brow and talked to him. "Do you have Faith Joe, She asked?" He nodded yes. Continuing, she quoted this Verse from the Bible to him: **"WHEN THOU LIEST DOWN, THOU SHALT NOT BE AFRAID: YEA, THOU SHALT LIE DOWN, AND THY SLEEP SHALL BE SWEET.** Now Joe, you just rest, go to sleep trusting in the Promise and Love of our Lord."

18
Chapter Eighteen

Chapter Eighteen

Joe was doing really well now. No infection had set in and he was able to stand for a long while. Sitting in a chair brought a rushing to his leg, but he did his best not to give in to it. After breakfast, nurse Shuman gave him the news he was waiting for. He was flying out tomorrow.

Suddenly he was running a gamete of emotions; excitement, fear, sorrow, happiness. It was like an old-fashioned pin-wheel blowing with the breeze. He kept thinking about Sarge and the squad. He felt helpless knowing the danger they were in, and now he was going home. He was told those feelings were normal, and often were accompanied by guilt. Well yes, that sounds just great, thought Joe, but textbook explanations couldn't see into the person's soul.

All the packing and getting his things together were done by the staff at the hospital, and Joe had taken time to write to the Military newspaper. He told of the wonderful care and devotion he had received. He wanted those who read it, soldier and civilian alike, to know how the wounded were getting the very best: in the worst of situations. When it came out the next month, he prayed it would bring comfort to those who had loved ones wounded like he was.

He was well attended each and every day, but a lot of the agony was brought on by hours of intermittent dressing and cleansing of his wounds. He had weaned himself off the powerful medications used to control the searing, nauseating, pain hitting his leg. He was not trying to be a hero or a martyr; he just didn't want to be dependent on them. Occasionally he did ask for relief but it was rare.

As Joe watched the sunrise, his thoughts were on Sarge, and all that he had done. He had found out Sarge had made two trips the day he was wounded. One was to carry him to safety, then go back to get Fella. He must have known it was too late to save their beloved dog. It was pure and unselfish love to retrieve him and not leave him. Joe had claimed Fella for his very own dog, and so did Sarge.

His heart ached so very much, but he was thankful they had time to show Fella he was not just a weapon of war. Thankful for the time to hug, pat, roll around the floor, and play with him. To make the soft, soothing night songs, which would make his ears, go up, turning his head almost sideways as he listened and watched their faces. Sometimes he would get so excited he would pounce like a rabbit. Memories of Fella brought Joe smiles and tears.

Before Joe knew it, the time had come. He was going first to a hospital for "rehab", then home. Nurse Shuman was there with a wheel chair, and some -where they had found a few balloons, which bounced and kept hitting him in the head. Calls of "good luck", "go with God", "eat a thick juicy steak" and the familiar "kiss the girls", echoed in his ears going down the hall.

Outside in the sun, Joe had to blink in the brightness. The hospital bus was waiting, along with two others also going home. Nurse Shuman was going along, to the plane, to monitor them. Joe was glad about that. Her enlistment was almost up and she wasn't sure if she would stay in the Service or go home herself. They promised to write once in awhile if possible.

It wasn't a long drive to the airfield, and mostly silence filled the bus. Each one lost inside with their private thoughts. The bus windows were painted over for protection of those inside. Joe could see through the front windows, with parts of the landscape showing the effects of bombs and land mines. He thought of this country he was leaving. The bleak empty stares of villagers, and the lost looks of the soldiers on both sides. There were silent figures lying on the ground. Oh Dear God, such a waste. Wars fought, and no one was ever the winner. And when it was over, thousands of lives lost, families left with only the sorrow of it all.

Joe could see the big transport plane ahead. When they finally stopped, the doors were opened and they began to unload. Equipment first, then one by one, they were helped off the bus. Placing him in a wheel chair, Nurse Shuman turned him to face the plane. Waiting alongside were two coffins, each draped with American flags. A full honor guard stood at attention. Joe took in the sight, catching his breath at the finality of the two going home to waiting families.

Joe looked to see signs of where Fella could be. He thought, he must be inside, waiting for me. Silently, to himself, he said, "I'm coming boy, we're going home together, like I promised".

As Joe and the others approached, they stopped a few feet away. Another one of the wounded, was going back with Joe, She was a nurse. They wheeled her to the front, along-side one of the coffins. She lovingly placed her hand on the closed lid. Stepping forward, soldiers formed on each side and prepared to fold the flag. Reading her a letter from the President of the United States, it said they both were being awarded medals. They presented them to her. Crying softly and holding her head up proudly, she leaned forward, kissing them and the coffin.

It was her brother that she was taking home, and clutching his flag to her chest, a purple heart was pinned on her hospital gown and one was placed on the flag for him. With all Saluting, she was gently lifted in one of the honor guard's arms, and carried into the opened door.

Joe was wheeled along-side the next coffin. A member of the Honor Guard stepped forward and began to read a letter, from the President of the United States, "Due to heroic actions on the battlefield, Cpl. Joseph Crocker, you have been promoted to the rank of Sergeant, with the gratitude of your Country". With that, he stepped forward and presented Joe with his new stripe, and pinned a Purple Heart on Joe. The surprise and honor sunk deep to the soul of Joe.

Stepping up again, he began to read another letter. "From the President of the United States, due to heroic actions on the battlefield, giving his life for his Country, Private F. Crogar has been promoted to the rank of Private First Class. To be given a Purple Heart and Meritorious Service Award posthumously. Being made aware that PFC Crogar, having no immediate or known family, with the place of birth the same as yours, I gratefully accept your offer to accompany him back home with you. That the burial has been arranged by you and Staff Sergeant Garrity".

Stepping back, the Honor Guard proceeded to fold the flag, handing it to Joe along with the medals. Joe leaned forward to speak, but the hand of nurse Shuman gently squeezed his shoulder. Leaning forward, she whispered to him, "Trust and remember you promise to Sarge, there is a letter waiting for you inside your seat".

With the ceremonies finished, it was time to leave. Joe was the last be boarded. Giving him a hug and a wave, the crying nurse Shuman turned, walking the empty wheel chair back to the bus.

Chapter Nineteen

On board, Joe was helped to his cot to prepare for take-off. Along with the ceremonies and ride there, he was drained. The pain in his leg was making his stomach churn, bringing the waves of nausea back. The doctor on board was ministering to the wounded. Checking Joe and redoing his bandages, he suggested a sedative along with a mild pain medication. He reminded Joe it was going to be a long flight; with two stops to refuel and possibly changing planes for the final one to the Hospital State side. Joe knew there wasn't a Military hospital at home, but one was not too far away.

His strength was sapped. His mind was on the ceremonies, and the awards. He couldn't stop thinking about the soldier he was taking back with him. Knowing another man from his home town, had died serving his Country, unsettled him. Had they met before, maybe gone to school together? He was sad that clear over here, he died. No family, no kin to be waiting for him, ever.

After some hot coffee and medication, pillows and blankets were distributed. Bundled up and warm, Joe reached to shift his weight a little and his hand found the letter from Sarge. He had forgotten all about it. Starting to open it, Joe felt tired and sleepy. He decided he'd wait until later to open the letter. His eyelids began to get heavy, and with the pain subsiding, he finally fell asleep.

Shaken nearly from his cot on the first landing, Joe was thankful someone had belted him in while he was sleeping. He suddenly was very hungry and as he was thinking about food, a tray suddenly appeared. The Core man helped him sit up and he ate every single bite. Who wouldn't: a thick juicy steak and all the trimmings, the topper being batter-fried onion rings. He wanted to thank everyone but they all were busy adding equipment on to the plane and making sure all was secure.

Joe craned his neck to see if the young nurse was all right. She was closer to the front, lying on her side. The engine and machinery noise made conversation nearly impossible. He yelled ahead to her and asked if she needed anything. Raising her head, and looking his way, she shook her head "no" and gave him the thumbs up. Joe bent his head in Prayer for her and her family.

He had Pa's Bible tucked inside his hospital shirt. Nurse Shuman, while wrapping the wounds on his chest, encased it in gauze and taped it on his other side of his body, away from the Protective covering of the sterile padding. Instead of it being hard or bulky, it brought comfort to him. Touching it with his hand, he thought about Fella again. Looking toward the cargo area, he saw nothing recognizable. He tried to get the attention of anyone who passed him. They weren't ignoring him, just finishing preparations to take off. Joe didn't mean to get impatient, but he had a sinking feeling that somehow Fella wasn't here with him. Joe's insides churned thinking they forgot Fella, and that he was all by himself, stuck somewhere, waiting for Joe.

Lying back down, the take off was smooth. Adjusting his bedding, the letter from Sarge was under his pillow. He had almost forgotten it was there, with so much going on and his concern about Fella. He opened it and began to read.

Dear Sergeant Joe:

Yes, I know about your promotion, I was told earlier. By now I pray you are well on your way. On board with you is a soldier named F. Crogar and you were asked to be his escort. It was very sad to think of him all alone and I knew you wouldn't mind. I would like to tell you something about this wonderful soldier and why he is important to the both of us.

The soldier in the *coffin* is our Fella. There was absolutely no other way to do it Joe. The paper work for him to go, as he was, was totally impossible to prepare in such a short time. I did nothing dishonest and you know me well enough to know that. I was asked to give his Name, Rank, and Serial Number, along with his family history etc. The clerk didn't even look at me face to face. He just sat there clicking away on his typewriter. When I hesitated, he told me to please hurry if I wanted him to make the plane on time.

I knew putting "Fella" as a first name wouldn't work. So the letter "F" became his First - Initial. He also needed a last name, and I took yours and mine, and combined them together. His Rank fitted him. He didn't mingle with anyone else unless ordered, except the squad. He was very lonely and "Private" until he became part of us. He was also "First Class" in every possible meaning. I had trouble with his serial number and again yours and mine worked. He had no Home Town that we knew of and now he does.

We were his family Joe, the only one he ever had. He deserved the promotion and service award. How could anyone who knew him even think his "Merit" was anything less than "Outstanding". There is no way to measure Fella, Joe. We both know that. He not only gave to his country, he gave you and me his heart, his love and his life.

I miss him too, and my heart hurts deeply as yours does. Each of us made a silent promise to him and kept it.

Your Pa and Sara will drive him home from the small airport outside of town. I called them. They know all about Fella and what happened to you both. Your Pa says he knows just where to bury him and that you would know also. They also said they would wait for you to call them if you want them to come to the hospital. They both love you Joe. Knowing your Faith and heart, you will encourage them to be with you as soon as the doctors say it's all right.

There you have it, my friend. Now you know why I had so little time to visit with you the day I left. Tonight, with each of us in our separate place, will pray for each other, and for this world always in conflict. We are both in God's hands, Joe. Someday soon, we will join up at the swamp, and we will rest, and be filled with our night songs. Write me when you can and I will do the same.

See you soon my friend, my brother.

Mark

Joe read the letter three times. He thought he couldn't weep anymore. It seemed as though this was all he had done for so long. He was never ashamed of tears, from man or woman. His Pa had explained tears came from a heart that was tender and caring, so again, they fell again from him. Sarge had asked him to trust and have Faith about Fella.

On board, was a casket carrying a young nurse's brother, and she, up in front of the plane, sharing her sorrow with God. Joe was in the back, with a casket carrying Fella, also sharing his sorrow. What is this "loss" that wounds the heart so? Joe laid there thinking of the ones who gave everything they had, that none would be lost. Even a sparrow that fell did not go un-noticed. Joe knew life, of every kind, had a meaning and importance to God.

In the privacy of Joe's heart and mind he gave thanks for Sarge's fulfillment of a kept promise. He also humbly gave thanks of the Promise "I will never leave you nor will I forsake you". Joe turned on his side, the letter in his hand, the Word in his heart.

Chapter Twenty

Joe had been in rehabilitation now for three months but he was improving a little too slow for him. Pa and Sara had lovingly laid Fella to rest. Pa didn't have to specifically tell Joe where he was going to bury Fella because he knew in his heart where that would be, and could picture it in his mind. His wounded leg was almost healed, and although he was aware the bottom half wasn't there any longer, it still hurt.

Joe was having trouble with "flashbacks", and there were nights he would be back at the "Front" fighting with his squad. Some nights it would be of Fella, jumping, bouncing around, taking the soldier down in the mess hall. Mostly it was of himself stopping for that last hug, hearing the "click" and feeling the weight of Fella's body on his. He saw the faces of those lying still in the dirt and mud and he would wake up stifling his screams, bathed in sweat. He was getting excellent counseling, and the others that had also been wounded, were a big help. They would gather a few at a time, talking about what had happened to them-selves. Some would think this was a detriment, but it helped to know others were going through similar things.

Pa had visited Joe once a week. It was a fairly long bus trip, but he needed Joe and the "need" went both ways. Talking on the phone with Sara was a nightly occurrence but she never pressured him to let her come to visit. After the last visit from Pa, they had a particularly long talk about that. Joe admitted he was afraid to meet her, to have her see him for the first time, the way he was now.

Pa was not one to get impatient or even hint at losing his temper, that was, until this time. With a slight edge to his voice, he reminded Joe that the world didn't revolve around his leg or his selfish attitude. Sara was at home; waiting to meet the man she loved and wanted to marry. If Joe wasn't interested, then be honest and let her go. Too many men wanted to get to know, and perhaps, even love Sara, but she had kept to herself, waiting for him.

Pa was disappointed with Joe and asked him if the war had taken all the love away from him? Then Pa saw the Bible, "his" Bible, which had saved Joe's life. "Is this just a book you keep on a table, moving around, out of the way?" The question brought Joe up sharply. "Have you quit believing all that you grew up with your whole life? Every breath you have ever drawn has been based on the truth of these words and teachings".

"This Book is love. Unselfish, and freely given for the asking. You ask for love, but you don't, or won't give it. You can be a whole man, or half a person. It looks like you have chosen the latter. I love you Joe, the "inside" of you, not the shell that encases your body. I want to pray with you now before I leave. You don't need help with the sole of your missing foot; you need help with the missing Soul of your whole being.

What happens to you from now on will be between you and God. You have decisions to make that will affect the rest of your life. A life that was given and known of, before you were born. You are my son but you are His child. All the morals and values you've learned have come from this Book. I'm going to go back and wait for you to come home Joe, to the swamp, to Sara, and to the night songs. Come home Joe, to Him". Kneeling on the hard concrete floor, Pa took "their" Bible, and pressing it to him, he held Joe's hand in his.

Struggling a little, Joe fitted his prosthesis carefully on the still, tender, knee cap. He had been using it for two weeks. A few blisters had formed, and it made walking uncomfortable, but the pain wasn't as bad as he thought it would be.

Glancing at the clock, he saw he was late. Waiting for him at the mess hall was his Sara. After his talk and prayer with Pa, Joe came face to face with himself. He didn't like who, or what, he had become. He wasn't even aware of how far he had wandered away from God. It had slipped up on him so quickly. To think of how close he came to forgetting His Grace, made him shudder.

Walking closer to her, Joe smoothed his hair for the fifth time. Coming through the door, her back was to him and she was sitting down. They were going to eat lunch together, and then she would catch the late bus back home. He wondered if she was as nervous as he was. Walking around the table, he pulled out a chair and sat down quickly.

Looking face to face, Joe thought she was the most incredibly beautiful woman he had ever seen. Her "doe" shaped eyes had the longest lashes he'd ever seen. Swallowing and catching his breath at the same time, he started to cough and choke. When he finally quit, he knew his face was bright red. Starting to talk, not only did he babble, but he also stuttered.

"What is wrong with me, Joe thought. She's going to get up and run away". Breaking into a full -blown laugh, Sara said, "Thank you, I thought it would be me doing something dopey first". Smiling at each other, their hands met at the same time across the table, and conversation flowed so fast and smooth, their words almost crossed over each other.

Not only was their meeting known by everyone there, the mess hall was almost packed by curious well wishers. Their meal was served to them, rarely done except for visiting dignitaries. They both knew they were being watched, but were so engrossed in each other that it didn't bother them. Their "waiter" brought dessert plus coffee for Joe, and tea for Sara, in cups and saucers. She thanked him for his kindness saying "this is the finest restaurant and service I've ever had" and the way she said it, it was sincere, and full of gratitude.

It was only when hearing the swishing of mops, the clatter of pots and pans, did they realize they were the only two left, still sitting in the mess hall. Looking at her watch, Sara let out a little gasp. She only had an hour to catch her bus and neither wanted the day to end.

Slowly Joe got up and pulled Sara's chair out for her. Reaching down a little, she put her hand a little way under her skirt. Joe heard the unusual sounds of snapping. Taking her other hand and looking down, he saw the braces. Sara's eyes were on Joe, and she said, "These are my everyday ones; you ought to see the ones I wear for dancing". Joe replied, with tears in his eyes, "We'll go dancing if I can lead, and it's a slow one".

In the Taxi, on the way to the bus stop, Sara told Joe of her life with Polio. Holding hands, they got out and walked to the bus. Looking into her eyes, Joe told her he loved her, and asked her to marry him. Saying yes, Sara told him she had prayed God would be with them this day and that if there were any doubt, she would know it. "I love you too Joe, I will come back to see you as much as I can. One day soon, we'll go home together, to the swamp and to our night songs".

Chapter Twenty-One

Yawning and repeating him-self, Joe said "Good Morning Shack", and looking into the mirror on his dresser, he glanced again at his slightly graying hair. Touching it, he wondered, where had the last eight years gone? Dressing quietly, he glanced over to his beautiful "bride" Sara, still sleeping. Slipping into the kitchen, he wanted her to sleep a little while longer before the children got up.

Putting on the coffee for Pa and himself, he also put the kettle on for tea for Sara. She still couldn't drink his strong brew, and when she did, she would put enough milk and sugar in it, that it was more like sweet hot milk. When she was expecting their first child, coffee made her stomach do flip- flops and usually she drank tea from then on.

Going out onto the back porch, which was now screened in, Joe sat down in his rocking chair. He took in the last few night songs that were still lingering. Smelling the finished coffee, he got himself a big cup, and sat down again. He was hoping for at least an hour for peace and quiet, before the giggling, noisy chatter would start. Sara didn't like to sleep too late, so he would wake her in plenty of time, before school. He thought he would also start the bacon and eggs, since there was no need to have both of them up right now.

Sara fared really well for the first two children. It was their last child, Debra, which caused a lot of complications. The weight of carrying the baby affected her legs so badly, that the last month before delivery, she was in bed most of the time. Sara was not one to have to "stay put" for very long, so she really had to pray for patience, that she wouldn't be grumpy and cross with the rest of her loved ones.

Debra was now five years old and had started school. Sara told Joe last night she had so much spare time, she didn't know what to do with herself. That made him laugh. He knew while he was at work she barely sat down. He would look at her swollen legs in the evening and know what a hard job it was, keeping up with all she had to do in the house. Then there was her volunteer work at the school two days a week, filling in at various jobs at church also. He would fuss at her and she would laughingly fuss right back at him. Her beautiful lilting laugh would melt his heart.

To Joe, every day was more beautiful with her in his life. He often thought of their wedding day. Married in the meadows of the swamp, and seemingly packed full with family and friends, there must have been over one hundred people.

It was an old fashioned ceremony with the reception right there, under the slow waving willows and the big towering moss covered trees. Tables were laden with food brought by everyone. Their wedding cake was a gift from the town baker. He had held Sara in his arms when she was so sick with Polio, so a cake from anyone else just wouldn't do.

While they were eating their cake, Joe remarked there were too many of Sara's 'old' suitors invited, and that was all Pa had to hear. Standing and tapping his cider glass, he announced that Sara needed to get a good look at all her former hopefuls, to make sure she didn't make a mistake. That brought about ten men forming a line, stopping in front of her, twirling around for her to see. Batting her long lashes at Joe, she made one or two come-backs for a repeat performance. Leaning over to Joe, she whispered, "I have to make sure I don't leave here with the wrong one for my honeymoon".

The only one missing was Sarge. He and his lovely wife were waiting for his discharge. His marriage was a surprise to everyone because he had called his folks the day before the wedding. They were going to her Parents home to have a small ceremony. He had wanted Joe to know that she was someone they both knew. He said he was not about to let her slip away from him, and was not like the 'snail' Joe was. He sent his love and said they would be home in about two weeks.

When Joe got the news he kept slapping Pa's back. Good old Sarge and Major Defore. He knew they had been friends, but he had no idea they had fallen in love. Joe couldn't wait. He and Sarge were going into business together. They both had a love for cabinet making, and the town needed good craftsmen. Finding the right building and all the details were worked out after Joe got back from his own honeymoon.

There were almost as many people at the train station as were at Sara and Joe's wedding. There was to be a big reception in the meadows for them. Pulling up, Sarge bounded off the train, amidst cheers and applause. Down came the red cap with their luggage. Sarge reached up and with their hands entwined, helped his lovely wife down the steps. Joe just about fainted. Letting out "oh boy, I don't believe it", Joe took both of them in his arms, and danced them around until they were all dizzy.

A puzzling hush fell over the crowd. Jumping up on a huge pile of suitcases, Sarge said in a booming voice, "Ladies and Gentlemen, Family and Friends, let me introduce my lovely wife, Abby Shuman". A giant roar went up.

Almost everyone there had heard of nurse Shuman, and all she had done for Joe. The times she had helped him and comforted Sarge too. The whole town knew she also helped bring Fella home. They were both engulfed in hugs and welcomes. Looking at Sara, Joe knew she had been in on the whole surprise and didn't tell him.

Picking Sara up in his arms and whirling her around, they fell in a heap of laughter and tears. Joe cushioned their landing and neither was hurt. Trying to be heard over the noise, she said, "are you angry with me? Mark asked me not to tell you". "No, my beauty, this was a wonderful surprise. I wouldn't have had it any other way". Everyone around reached out to help them up and brush them off, and the ride to the meadows was joyous for all of them.

After the reception and the guests had left, Joe, Sara, Sarge, Abby and Pa went to view Fella's grave. The two miles to the site was a silent one. Joe made sure Sara wasn't getting fatigued, and they stopped their walk to rest, several times. Coming around the bend was a calm, serene area. They had all been there before, except Mark and Abby. It wasn't far from Pa's private place of Prayer. Only a few had been there; it was a place not shared by many.

It was getting close to dusk, about two hours before sundown. Coming to a small mound and a headstone, they held hands and stood in front, facing it. Tears were falling, not held back by anyone. Their beautiful, brave Fella, was not where he should be. He deserved to be running, prancing and walking by their sides.

Sarge wanted to say something but couldn't, so Joe looked at his Pa. He knew, in times of seeking wisdom and comfort, God had always shown Pa what to do and say. Pa stepped forward to face the small mound, now covered with glistening dew in the twilight. "I have stood here, in this place, before you, many times our Heavenly Father.

Often it's just you and I, but today, a most grateful Blessed Family kneel in humble Thanksgiving and love.

The last ones to know Fella have come home, by your Grace. Many brave men and women in times past have been lost in the battles of war. Loved ones have gathered around in similar places, to feel Your loving arms of comfort. Hearts broken and bowed down in sorrow. Many Father, have fallen and remained where they fell. You were with them all. The circle is complete for Joe, Mark, Fella and You. Thank you for sending Fella to be with them, and the soldiers he came in contact with. Many returned home to their loved ones because of him. You gave him a heart, once ruthlessly filled with fear and loneliness, and replaced all of that with Your Majesty. Every breathing creature you created, need You, there is nothing on this earth that you have not made. We are humbled to praise Your Name. Amen".

Every one departed, each lost in their own thoughts. Joe hugged his Pa for a long time. Pa gave the keys to the car to Joe saying he wanted to stay in his 'special place' for a little while alone. Sarge and Abby said they would see them in a day or two. Sarge wanted his family to visit with Abby for a while before the two of them started to settle in.

As Sara and Joe drove home to the swamp, they had the windows down to feel the soft sweet air on them. Walking up to the shack, they stood looking at the setting sun. There were brilliant colors of Reds, Gold's, and Purples, with billowing clouds reflecting their glow on the waters of the swamp. With their arms around each other they went in. Just as the night songs began.

22
Chapter Twenty-Two

Chapter Twenty- Two

Joe was busy cooking breakfast when the children came bouncing in from their bed -rooms. Noisy chatter filled the kitchen. Sara had finished setting the table. Joe loved watching her moving around the house. She had a way of filling each room with warmth and beauty. The children were excited because tomorrow was a holiday from school. Both families of Joe and Sarge were planning that day with fishing and picnics. Joe was glad to have some time like this.

With work and family time, he had something to talk to Sarge about. It wasn't a problem exactly, it was something he had seen in the swamp, or thought he had seen. The children hustled, gathering their School -work and lunches because the bus would be there any minute. Sara walked out with them, caught up in their laughter. It was time for Joe to go into town to work. He and Sarge had purchased a little shop, and turned it into a fine place for cabinet making. They didn't lack for any work because word had spread of their fine craftsmanship, so usually they had back orders of people wanting their wares.

Now with school over for the day, the children got busy with their chores. On one of the kitchen shelves, there was the famous 'Job Jar'. Sunday evenings they would get it down and all would sit at the kitchen table, and even Pa came for his part. Inside held small slips of paper, and on each slip was a job that needed to be handled for the week ahead. They each took turns picking out the slips until the jar was empty, this way one person wouldn't have the same chore all the time. It also taught the children to do the jobs that were theirs, differently, if they wanted to. They all thought this was fair, all except Mary Rose.

Expectant eyes would look at her and wait. Sure enough, she would protest most of the jobs she had drawn. Taking out the garbage brought out most wails of "it's too stinky or too far to walk". Much laughter arose from that table on 'Job Jar' night. Pa would get many laughs, even from Mary Rose. If he drew dish-washing, he would hop around pretending to wring his hands, faking a cry that his 'pretty' hands would get all wrinkled.

Little Sam would be the next, and even though he was the middle child, he was already taller than Mary Rose. Drawing laundry details brought him rushing out on the back porch with a big basket on his head, and invariable it would fall off hitting something. Sunday nights were pretty raucous and Abby was happy they had no close neighbors to hear all the noise.

With Mary Rose and Sam finishing the kitchen chores for the evening, Sara and Joe sat out on the back porch taking in the beauty of the swamp. Little Debra sat down on the big rug by their rocking chairs. She was folding socks and under clothes, fresh from the clothe line. That was one of her "drawn" jobs. Humming softly, she was doing well with her little fingers. Pa had taken out the 'stinky' trash and was in his room getting the fishing gear ready for the big day tomorrow. Sooner or later all the children would end up in his room.

Pa would spend his evenings reading the Bible to them or telling them tall tales. He also patiently worked with each one on fishing tackle, showing them how to tie hooks and anything else they wanted to know. On nights when they had homework, Pa sat on the porch or would get in the dugout and pole for a while. Sometimes Joe, Sara or one of the children would join him. They had several dugouts now and the children were getting very good at 'poling', Debra hung on, her hands down toward the bottom of the pole with the adept hands of one of the adults up at the top.

Joe would catch Sara watching Debra at times. Asking her why she did that, she simply said she wasn't much older than Debra when she came down with Polio and was thankful the children in this country had medicine to prevent it. She never seemed angry or upset that she had been so sick and Joe asked her about it that night. Sara let her head lean on the back of the rocking chair. Answering Joe's question seemed easy for her. "I never gave having Polio a thought. There were so many of us, not only here in this small town but all over the country. I was one of the luckier ones. We still have one from here, living in an iron lung in a "Special" hospital. He is clear across the state."

Hearing Sara mention someone in an iron lung, Joe stopped rocking. could it be possible his old childhood friend and hers were the same? In their continued talk, not only was it possible, it was true. They both knew him and had gone to school with him, a different year and grade. Sara's family had visited him several times before he was transferred there. They sat talking of how they could have missed seeing each other during those times.

More amazing that they each wrote letters to him and his family, even now. Neither made the connection as they mailed those letters during their marriage. Joe knew him as a vibrant fishing friend and Sara knew him as a struggling Polio friend. It was his sweet nature and loving heart that endured him to all.

Another connection for Sara and Joe was that Joe would sit at work, on his lunch hour, writing his letters, and getting replies there. Sara, at home, was doing the same. Their friend Phillip and his family never knew the name Crocker was from the same family. Each had known him in circumstances unlike the other and their visiting and letter writing was so separate no one knew. Not until now. He will really enjoy knowing his two friends were 'one' and been for quite awhile.

Sara and Philip, were just a few miles away from Joe. Lives ravaged by a relentless disease with pain encompassing them and their families. Joe and Pa were living their lives secluded, being comforted in the swamp, God's beauty surrounding them every day.

Joe hung his head, filled with sorrow, even guilt. "Even now Sara, you don't see those times as filled with hurt and pain. I was here, enjoying life in the swamp, you and Phillip were living your lives wracked with pain. Never once have I heard you complain about your life"

"Joe, Philip and I fought a private battle and war with sickness that attacked our bodies. You fought a public battle, where thousands died. If you could have stopped either one, you would have and so would have I. It wasn't up to us Joe. God loved us and used us as He determined. He decided our lives Joe, not us. We pray for strength, courage and wisdom to serve Him, His way. He loves us all, not wanting anyone to suffer. One day we will be with Him, healed, alive and filled in His Glory. We must lift our heads up Joe, not down".

I drove my Ma and Pa crazy playing sports. I liked softball best and couldn't run fast, but I was a champion at sliding. Poor Pa would have to take my braces all apart after a game, just to get all that dirt out of the hinges. When we played in the mud, I just sort of snuck in the back door, sat in a chair and waited for him to explode. He never did though, most of the time He would take each hunk of mud, and layer it on my face".

Sara's soft laughter floated through the swamp. "You have to admit I also had an advantage when I rocked our babies during the middle of the night. If dozed off my legs were locked in place so they didn't roll off onto the floor". That got her laughing again and even Debra joined in their revelry. "See there, Poppa, Momma's legs are pretty fine after all!" Little Debra watched her parents exchanging their shared love. She had heard the words of pain and sorrow. Going to them she said "I'm sorry Momma, your legs were hurt and Poppa, your heart was hurt. I think God hurts too. I know I'm still little, but I will try real hard to keep smiles here, do you think that will make God smile?" Picking her up in his arms, Joe was already smiling. "**A little child shall lead them**" and the Scriptures speak truth always Debra. Yes, you always bring smiles, making hearts happy, all of our hearts". Gathering the folded laundry, they helped her to take them inside.

Morning came sooner than Joe and Sara wanted. The children were up and raring to get going. They laid there listening to the whispered talk in the kitchen. The children had gotten cereal for themselves and were trying their best to be quiet. They both agreed long ago that they were truly blessed. Their children were kind and considerate, not only to them but to others, as well. Most of the children they knew, in their area, were also decent, honest and well brought up. Sara was so thankful that Joe's Pa lived with them. He was a wonderful influence, not only for the children but for them as well.

Joe smelled the coffee brewing and knew Pa was up and about too. The years had gone by so quickly. As he was getting dressed, Joe thought back to the first day they had driven up to the shack. Pa was so strong, yet gentle. Working hard to make a wonderful life for Joe; He was always putting himself last, bearing a lot of sorrow, yet praising God always. Tears welled up in Joe's eyes. Pa, now slightly stooped, was forever giving, not taking.

Walking into the kitchen, Joe hugged his Pa a little extra hard. Hugs were as much a part of their household as breathing was. If they all went too long without one, they would stop whatever they were doing, and go looking for the nearest neck they could find. "You know what Pa? I forgot to tell you this morning, my heart is your and always will be. Not only am I blessed to have you as my Pa, I thank you for bringing me to the Lord". Standing quietly in the doorway, Sara thanked God for her family here in this home; giving thanks that her parents, brothers and sisters were also bonded in faith.

Joe was anxious to see Sarge. Something had been happening to him. He knew if anyone could make sense of it, it would be him. Gathering the family and the food baskets, they set out for the meadows. Most of the get-togethers were held there. This was such a beautiful day, Warm with morning dew lifting gently off the Earth. Birds flying and swooping down for the things needed to build their nests. Joe was amazed that God gave them the knowledge to know just what each kind needed for their building materials. Everyday things that people take for granted, were right before their eyes.

By the time they arrived there, the meadow was filled with laughter and children running around playing, Adults were setting up the tables with food and fishing gear was taken down by the water.

With so many family members, cleaning up the leftover food, after eating, didn't take long. The men folded the tables, loading them on the back of the trucks. Now on to fishing which brought cheers by all. There were enough dugouts and they quickly filled up. Often, family members used the dugouts for talks, plans and much needed pondering.

Away from the hectic days and lives they all were soothed by the peace of the swamp. Joe poked Sarge in the ribs saying, "have you noticed our Sons, Sam and Gabe this past week? They have their heads together, whispering all the time. Think they're plotting something?" Sarge looked over his shoulder at the two and nodded. "Sara said they get off the bus chattering; quickly finish their chores and meet down the road, ending up in deep talk. Guess we'll find out soon enough".

Poling through the water, Joe and Sarge passed a few small boats with putt-putt motors. More and more were fishing the area. Lakes nearby got the bigger noisier boats and they were thankful for that. Getting good fish was harder now that the area had begun to be built up. The best places to fish could only be found by dugouts and the locals knew the inner swamp, gliding in and out silently. The noise hadn't gotten too bad yet, but they all knew it was a matter of time.

Finding the spot they were looking for, poles were laid down and they sat back, wrapped up in the peace and quiet. Sarge broke the silence by asking Joe what was on his mind. "Well, I know we've talked some about flash-backs and dreams of the war. Time has helped me a lot plus prayer. About two weeks ago I was by myself poleing. I thought I saw a flash or a movement behind some bushes. I kept watching until it disappeared. Mark, it looked like a dog; just like Fella. It's happened twice since then. Once, in the meadows and again, close to the shack. I even called out. Whatever it was, stopped and then went on. It really looked just like him, same coloring and build. I know he's gone and I also know sometimes the mind can manufacture things we miss or need. I asked around town and no one has a dog like that. This "vision" has me concerned. Should I go back to the hospital? Have you seen anything or had feelings like this?

Sarge took a moment before answering him. "You've thrown a lot at me you know. I've had my share of "visions" or flash backs too. I was sent back to the fighting after you got hurt. Even now that the War is over, the dreams continue. I see and hear things that come upon me at times I can't control. We've both broken out in the sweats, our hearts beating so fast it's like a heart attack. There's not a Veteran of any War that doesn't continue doing this particular thing. It's similar to putting your hand in wet cement: when dried, the outlines are still there.

Fella is imprinted within us, more for you than for me. You were the first he came to trust and love. He slept, drank and ate with you. He even seemed to pray with you. I watched him when you would be on your knees praying. He would lie down besides you, putting his head between his paws. I never told you about that, it was too private.

I think you saw something here. It could have been a swamp deer or cougar. I personally don't think you need to go back to the Hospital but it's a decision you have to make. Faith has always sustained us Joe, Let's Pray for an answer. It had been almost a week since his conversation with Sarge.

23
Chapter Twenty-Three

Chapter Twenty-Three

With no more "Sightings", he talked to Sara and Pa about it. He and Pa went out each evening, but they saw nothing. Joe was feeling much better, so later, after supper they all prayed about it, even the children. They always discussed things that were important. Happenings in life needed Prayer and joining hands together also joined their lives.

Little Sam was unusually quiet. Normally he had thoughts to share, but on this matter he said nothing. He and Gabe were still putting their heads together in private conversations. Pa had mentioned, to Sara and Joe that several times Sam had taken a chair, reached up to the top shelf over the sink, and borrowed his Bible. He had one of his own, as all the children did. Pa thought just maybe there was some significance in some way to his behavior.

Sara remarked, in talking with Abby, that Gabe had a lot on his mind also. Later in the week when Joe got home from work, Sara met him at the door with a worried look on her face. Sam had come home, did his chores, and now couldn't be found. She and Pa called for him but he never came. Joe went out and couldn't find him either. Sara already had spoken to her brother to see if Sam was there. Mark said he was already on his way to their house. Gabe was there at Mark and Abbey's home but was crying and seemed frightened. After some questioning, Gabe told Mark he would find Sam, and bring him home to Joe and Sara's. He knew just where to find him. Knowing the two boys were safe, both families were sitting in the kitchen waiting for them. The back porch door opened and in came the two boys, hand in hand. Faces smeared with dirt and tears.

Little Sam handed Joe a letter, his whole body shaking. "Poppa, I have something really important to tell you, I have sinned. I took the "Special" Bible. Gabe and I keep looking for the right Scriptures and we thought your Bible was more important than ours. It's not his fault Poppa, he kept telling me to go straight to you and Momma, but I didn't. My heart hurts hard. I want to do the right thing, but I don't know how. I'm sorry".

Joe put his arms around Sam, put him on his lap, and began to read the letter that was handed to him.

"Hello, we are a family staying in your town. It's a temporary stop while we look for work. Part of our family is our pet, Dakota. She gave us a surprise we hadn't planned on: We kept one and the other one took to your son's school. He's a nice boy and the puppy wanted nothing to do with anyone other than your son. He told us he couldn't have her and left.

Two days we came to the school but the puppy wouldn't cotton to anyone else. She's weaned already, but has refused to eat for us. After a few more days, out of desperation for her safety and health, we took her back to the school. Sure enough, as soon she saw your boy, she gulped down her food, and ended up on his lap, until recess was over. He said he would ask you again, and let us know the next morning as fate would have it, that night we were offered a job in another State.

On our way out of town, we stopped at the school. We thank you for changing your mind about the pup. The two of them seem to have a bond. Sam mentioned you shared something special with a dog in your life too.

We have been worried about the Mother. Several times she just took off on us. On those nights she came home covered with mud and gooey slime. We figured she was out in the swamp area but the strange part is, she's a city dog, and never liked the water. Giving her a bath takes the two of us plus the children, so we're off now, thanks again for taking her. Those two are a pair, that's for sure. God be with you and yours.

Respectfully,

Mr. Charles Farnsworth."

Joe, Sarge, and Pa exchanged glances, remembering the 'vision' Joe had seen earlier. Standing up again, Sam continued, "they just left Poppa". There I was, holding this pup, them talking about going and she would be gone. I lied to them, saying you said we could have her. I hid her, ran and got Gabe. We put her under my shirt on the bus. We fixed a place for her back toward the meadow. Gabe and me took turns giving her our lunch, and then we would share whatever was left.

She's been real good Poppa. She stays right where I tell her until I get back to her. She's smart too, we hide stuff and in no time, she finds it". Starting to cry again and taking a breath, "I was bringing her home today to show you. Me and Gabe know God is all about love so would read your Bible trying to find the right words. We were really careful turning the pages, Poppa, You told us someday you would tell us why the holes are there. I even put it to my heart like I see you Poppa, while you are praying. You look real peaceful holding it, so we knew reading the Bible would really help. Most times love was talked about.

Today when I started to pick her up she growled at me. She was looking by my ankle and there was a big snake, all coiled up, coming at me. Next thing she hit the head of the snake with her feet as it struck at me. Momma, there's two holes in my school pants. If you show me how, I'll fix them real good. I know we can't keep her. But leaving her alone, out by herself, she's goanna get hurt or killed. I need help Momma and Poppa".

The kitchen was real quiet. Most eyes were on Joe. Nodding his head up and down a little, Joe wiped Sam's face. "Why don't all you children go back yard and in the play while we talk about it." Faster than you could shake a stick, they were gone. They didn't know whether to laugh or cry. There were lessons here for all ages. Pa put on some coffee and also the teapot. "How will you handle it, Pa asked, throwing the question to both sets of parents."

Abby was the one first to speak. "Seems like a long time ago I met two men, and their hearts were brought together by a dog. Them being a bit older didn't diminish the truth, that they both loved him. From what I was told then, that dog loved no one else the way he did them. An ugly horrible war took him away before they had a chance to shower him with all the love they had inside. He was a loner, doing a job taught him. One beautiful, blessed time, God's Grace gave him a family. It was short lived, but at least he had one".

Sara broke the silence this time. "Each one of the children knows about deception. They have been brought up with God's principles. They're out in that yard realizing how that puppy came here. They know something that seems so right, was gotten in the wrong way". Clearing his throat, Sarge said, "We certainly have a problem here. Keeping a puppy you know you weren't suppose to have, isn't a life threatening disaster. For those youngsters though, there is a life Honesty lesson here.

What's your opinion on this, looking directly toward Pa." Joe's Pa was quietly sipping his coffee, listening to what was being said. "All I know is, how I was raised and what I tried to install in Joe. I'm going to give this back to you son. I've watched you and Sara bring up these babies. You both have done a good job, a job I'm very proud of."

Putting his arm around Sara, Joe called the boys back inside and to bring the Puppy too. All of the children started filing in slowly, with Gabe, Sam and the wiggling bundle of fur in tow. Sitting around in a circle, Sam turned the puppy around to face them. Sarge let out a gasp of air, scaring the children and everyone else. Joe looked at the puppy, and tears welled up in his eyes. He had to take a minute to clear his throat. "We understand Sam, that a problem can be pushed right at us, and we only have a minute or two sometimes, to make a decision. When we have no one to go to for help, we do the best we can: Even if it's a big mistake. You and Gabe looked to the Scriptures for the answer and that's the most important and right thing to do. We have failed you also, you and Gabe. We thought we had taught all of you children that you could come to us. To trust that with Faith, we would do our best not to judge you before hearing what was on your minds. Do not be afraid of us. We serve God and He uses us to teach, love, instruct and help you.

We are here to show you where to find answers in the Bible, and it doesn't matter whose one you use. They are our Instructions before leaving this earth. Just as we read the leaflets that come with things that have to be put together, that is what the Bible is. Putting our lives together following His guidance. We are going to get tablets for each of you to write on. When words such as Trust, Fear, Belief, Guidance and others come to your minds, and you want to make sure you know just what they mean, you write these down and we will help you find where they are in the Holy Word. When you are afraid or confused, come to us and with God's Grace, we will work it out as a family. Do you all understand what I am saying and what I mean?" Little heads all over the room bobbed up and down, and their stiff shoulders relaxed.

"Samuel, you gave this creature from God your heart. She's placing her trust that you will treat her kindly, with love. There will be many animals that come to our homes, and we can't take them all in. We can try to find homes to suit each one. Some are here for a just a short time and then wander away. Some animals have barriers against human love and they don't stay because cruelty has hurt them.

There are needs and wants in life. God will supply all your "Needs". The "Wants" may never happen, and that's something only God, in His Wisdom, will determine. This puppy no one wanted or needed. Her owners put in a lot of time trying to "make" her choose just anyone, but something in her heart made her love the two of you.

We will never understand just why or how that happened, only God knows. "Have you two given her a name?" asked Sarge. Sam replied, "We call her Tracker. It's not really for a girl but you just can't hide anything or anyone from her. Thinking for a minute, Joe said "it's a fine name and we are most thankful to God that she saved you both from that snake. Find a box and get her settled on the back porch. She's going to be a pretty big when she's grown, and she will be a good watch -dog.

"We are going to make some hot chocolate for you all and then it's on to bed. It's late now, and don't forget there's school tomorrow". Sam and Gabe hit Joe so hard with hugs that the puppy nearly was crushed in between. Laughing children filled the yard and porch. Debra got her baby blanket, Mary Rose got some old ripped socks for her to play with. Meanwhile, Tracker ran back and forth, bouncing like a rabbit, all the while, jabbing Sam on his ankle. While Sara and Abby were mixing the drinks, they fixed some sandwiches. They suddenly were famished.

Pa set the table saying, "all right, I don't know if it was just me, but seeing that pup clearly affected the both of you. What's going on?" Both men started to talk at the same time. Not to Pa specifically, words pouring forth all mingled together. "Whoa -there, I don't understand gibberish so well".

Sarge said, "She's just like Fella. It's not so much the coloring, and I can't put my finger on just what it is". Grinning and hugging Sara, Joe said, "It's her eyes. The color, the shape, and the look, that pierces the core of your heart. There will never be another Fella, but this little girl takes hold, that's for sure. No wonder the boys couldn't walk away. I pray we did right for all".

With the children tucked safely in bed, they prayed with each child at their bedsides. Tracker had her place on the porch, and Joe had asked Pa if he had done the right thing. Pa told him to search his heart and give it to the Lord in prayer, that he was very proud of all of them. Saying good night, he left Sara and Joe sitting in the kitchen Sara walked over and peeked out the window for the third time. "What is she doing now? asked Joe. "Well, she is still standing there looking at the door-knob. I don't think she has laid down at all. Are you thinking what I'm thinking?" Giving Sara a hug, "We'll just put the box next to Sam's bed. That ought to do it". Gathering her bed and things, they carried her in and settled her down. Joe still couldn't resist watching those beautiful eyes, a little bit of Fella. He was thankful that she had her own personality, similar but not the same. Nothing God created was a copy.

Getting into bed, Joe had difficulty falling asleep. Memories of Fella and the old tin box of years ago f filled his mind. How he had grown up that night, thinking that it would be filled with 'Fun' things. Pa never wanted to bring it out and talk about it, until Joe pestered him to show him. A glimpse of the future that Joe was sorry he ever saw. Now he used it for the same reasons Pa had: His medals, Fella's, and Pa's. The pouch Fella carried around his neck was in there also. The fireplace mantle Pa had made, while he was away, held the folded flag that was on his casket: Inside a special Oak glass lidded box Pa had made to hold them.

Hearing a thud, Joe got up quietly, not wanting to wake Sara. Walking toward Sam's room, he heard the thud again. Peeking in, Tracker was trying to jump up on the bed, falling flat on her back each time. Joe sighed, picked her up, and placed her at the foot of the bed. Looking back at Joe with those big brown eyes, she promptly snuggled up against Sam's back. Turning around, there stood Sara. She had put on her heavy braces again and with arms crossed leaned against the door and watched. They walked back to their room and on their knees in Prayer, gave humble thanks and Praise for the never ending Love, Mercy and the Grace of God. From outside came the sounds of the night songs of comfort and peace.

~ THE END ~

Made in the USA